# Megan of the Mists

## by

## Bill Lockwood

This is a work of fiction. Names, characters, places, and incidents are either the product of the author's imagination or are used fictitiously, and any resemblance to actual persons living or dead, business establishments, events, or locales, is entirely coincidental.

**Megan of the Mists**

COPYRIGHT © 2017 by William B. Lockwood

All rights reserved. No part of this book may be used or reproduced in any manner whatsoever without written permission of the author or The Wild Rose Press, Inc. except in the case of brief quotations embodied in critical articles or reviews.
Contact Information: info@thewildrosepress.com

Cover Art by *Kristian Norris*

The Wild Rose Press, Inc.
PO Box 708
Adams Basin, NY 14410-0708
Visit us at www.thewildrosepress.com

Publishing History
First Vintage Rose Edition, 2017
Print ISBN 978-1-5092-1322-1
Digital ISBN 978-1-5092-1323-8


Published in the United States of America

**"Go quickly. Get in the seat behind them."**

Megan looked warily at the men. She did not move.

"Go quickly," Brian urged. He glanced around. "I'll be waitin' at the pub. I can't stay here long."

Megan gave a sigh. She got out of the truck and walked to the car.

The two men watched as she approached. The driver gestured toward the back seat with his head.

Megan got in and closed the door. She felt cramped in the back seat. The car smelled like stale cigarette smoke and beer.

The driver started the engine, and they moved quickly out into the crowded street. Brian had already pulled away.

The man in the passenger seat turned around. He handed Megan a balled-up piece of cloth. "Put this on, and keep your head down," he ordered.

Megan frowned. She spread the cloth out on her knee. "What is this?" she asked.

"Balaclava," the man answered.

"Oh, sure," Megan said. She recognized the traditional hood worn by the IRA to conceal their identity. She had never worn one for the jobs she did. She held it up to her face. It smelled of the sweat of many scared men.

"It'll mess my hair."

"Got some fight in her," the driver said. "And pretty too."

The other man looked around again. His unemotional eyes met her hard glare. "Eyeholes to the rear, dear. We'll find you a comb."

## Also by Bill Lockwood
## and available from The Wild Rose Press, Inc.
*BURIED GOLD*

After her father's death, thirty-something Evie steals a map from his home. The map is a principal lead to where a box of ten-dollar gold coins was buried during Prohibition, just before the Revenuers raided her grandfather's illegal rum-running business out on Long Island.

Evie, along with her teenaged daughter, Cindy, collects other clues, staying just a step or two ahead of her brothers, who are also after the treasure. Her search is complicated when one of the old-timers in the little town on Peconic Bay is murdered. As Evie desperately tries to track down key information to make the map work, she elicits the help of a local bartender and then that of Max, an old boyfriend. Getting rich is not easy.

~*~

"Lockwood writes with authority and keeps the reader rooted in the eighties with references to famous people, music, and more. He does not miss a single beat in *BURIED GOLD* whose main characters are Baby Boomers and Gen-Xers. …[T]he characters interact and move about with precision and the reader is firmly grounded in all aspects of movement, setting, and storyline. The dialogue is spot-on, too. The language is as diverse as the characters. Not only can I hear them, but I can see them, too. The characters each have their appropriate share of grace; their humanity is present and they appear in the flesh. In the end, isn't that what readers look for?"

~*Shelley Carpenter, Candle-Ends: Reviews,*
*Toasted Cheese Literary Journal*

## Dedication

To all the brave women who stood up against the violence in Northern Ireland.

# Author's Notes on History and Myth

Some historians date the struggle for Irish freedom to the Battle of the Boyne in Northern Ireland in 1690, when the Catholic forces of James II were defeated by the Protestant William the Conqueror, but resistance to an increase in British control may well date back to the assassination of Henry VIII's Irish Chancellor in 1534.

A Catholic rising in 1641 was cruelly put down by British soldiers of the Cromwell regime. About 12,000 of them were rewarded with free land in northeast Ireland, making an unpopular Protestant population. There were more Irish uprisings through the years, the major ones being in 1789, 1803, 1848, and, the best known, the Easter Rebellion of 1916. The Irish celebrated their rebellions in story and song that combined with the myths from the past of druids and fairies, making it all a very romantic thing. The singers, storytellers, and true rebels seem to know all the dates no matter how long ago. Large in the legends and mythology of the revolutions is the IRA (Irish Republican Army), an organization with a culture of secrecy and loyalty somewhere between a fraternal organization and the Italian Mafia in the US.

Negotiations followed the 1916 rebellion, and on December 6, 1922, the area in southern Ireland with a predominantly Catholic majority was formally established as the Irish Free State, today's Irish Republic. Protestant Northern Ireland remained part of the United Kingdom, under British control, and some elements of the Catholic minority there fought on. In the 1970s, riots, vengeance killings, and British repression rose to a frightening level. The fact that the problem was more a struggle for far too few jobs, divided on sectarian lines, rather than the old glorious fight for Ireland's freedom is a matter for the political scientists.

The Good Friday Agreement of April 10, 1998, negotiated with the help of the US government, appears to have calmed the violence for now. But in stark contrast to the brutality and violence experienced by those who lived it, for us Americans in the "Irish" bars of this country the revolution and ongoing struggle in Northern Ireland was in the 1970s as romantic as the fairy stories of old.

****

My middle name is Bayley, spelled an Irish way. It was handed down on my father's side, being his middle name and that of his father before. My aunt did some ancestral research and found a Henry Bayley (b. 1801, d. 1886), my great-great-grandfather. He immigrated to New York in 1828 and moved to Baltimore, MD. An obituary in the *Baltimore Sun* mentions that his father, and the father before him, were British officials in Cork, Ireland. I'm certain that fact won't endear me to the guys in the "Irish" bars of Long Island. And I have a degree in Political Science. Still, I love Irish rebel songs, their other folk music, their tales of fairies, and the stories, however they be myths, of old.

# Part One

# Ireland

## Armaugh, Monheghan, and the Border

> For the Great Gaels of Ireland
> Are the men that God made mad,
> For all their wars are merry
> And all their songs are sad.
> ~G. K. Chesterson

Chapter One

The young man put his suitcase down beside the litter can in the bus station. His heart pounded. An officer of the Royal Ulster Constabulary stood only ten feet away. His training had not covered such near proximity of the enemy. The young man hoped the officer would not notice the sweat that poured down his face. The air in the dingy station was heavy with humidity, but it was cool.

The young man started toward the door where the bus to Armaugh was about to arrive.

"Pardon me, sir," the officer said.

The young man spun around.

"Your case, sir. Did you leave it there by the can?"

"Oh," the young man said. He tried his best to act surprised.

The officer waited for more.

"I was going over to the door to see if the bus for Armaugh was coming," he added.

"Do you have a ticket?" the officer asked.

The young man had an inward sigh of relief. The first thing he had done when he entered the station was buy a ticket. His training had served him well on that account. He pulled it from his pocket and handed it over.

"I just wanted to see if the bus is coming," he repeated. "And I want to use the loo."

The officer looked at the ticket. As he did, the young man backed away. Halfway across the room he turned and ran for the door.

"Stop, you…" the officer shouted.

The young man burst through and ran past a British soldier who was standing guard outside. The officer was close behind.

"Stop him," he heard the officer shout. The bus was coming down the road.

"Stop, you!" the soldier shouted. "Stop, or I shoot."

The first shot was for warning. It was fired in the air. Before the second one, the young man hit the ground. Then he raised his head and looked back over his shoulder. He was just in time to see the bus station explode in a ball of flame.

The young man scrambled to his feet and ran away.

## Chapter Two

"The Brits were out with their helicopters today," Colleen said. "There was a bombing near Armaugh while you were sleepin' most of a Sunday away."

"Bugger the Brits," Megan said.

"My, aren't we in a good mood."

"Patty was three hours late with my pack," Megan complained. She hunched the straps of the dark blue backpack higher on her shoulders. She wore a thick black turtleneck sweater, dark jeans, and running shoes. Her long dark hair was tied back, and her face reflected only the weak starlight that was the sole illumination outside the farmhouse door. Despite their distance from the border, Colleen kept the inside lights off when Megan started her runs.

Colleen's features softened. Her hair hung loose, and she wore fuzzy slippers. "Sure you don't want another cup of tea before you cross over?" she asked.

"No," Megan said. "I'm already behind. I want to get it done. I have a long day tomorrow."

"Godspeed, then."

Megan smiled. "See you soon."

Then she ran out into the dark night.

The farmhouse door shut with a soft sound behind her.

Megan was alone with her backpack of contraband in the Irish countryside where she always crossed the border. She was between the town of Armaugh where she lived in the north and Monheghan in the south. She ran along through the trees under the faint light of all the stars.

"Sure, if Northern Ireland had an Olympic team, you'd be the star of it," both her mother and her boyfriend had said. It was the only thing she had remembered those two having ever agreed on.

Megan smiled. Her answer to her boyfriend had been, "I'm using my running talents for the nation already." To her mother she had said not a word.

Megan stopped. She caught her breath and listened for a minute or two. There was a chill in the night air. She knew there would be mist on the hills in the morning. Despite the wool socks, her feet were cold. Her own breathing was the loudest thing she could hear.

*No sounds of helicopters. Hopefully the bombing thing Colleen talked about is all over. I can't have the Brits looking in my woods for some runaway bomber.*

Megan looked over to her right, where she knew the ground rose in a kind of mound. "Protect me, please, again this night on my journey," she whispered to the little people that legend said lived there.

Then Megan ran on.

The ground dropped down, and she leaped a shallow stream. Then she went up again. At the top of a rise she stopped again.

She saw a pair of headlights ahead, passing through the trees. She knew the road ahead. She was over the border.

Megan waited for the car to pass well away. She shifted her shoulders against the weight of the backpack she was carrying, and again her mind drifted to the story of the day's bombing. "Do you ever wonder what's in those packs you carry over?" Colleen had once asked her. "They don't tell, and I don't ask," Megan remembered answering. Megan hunched her shoulders and pulled at the straps. This one was heavier than some. She also remembered her boyfriend saying, "Once you're with us, don't ever say no."

The car was gone. Megan ran on.

She reached the road, and she ran along the side by a long high hedge that continued for a distance. She reached a break, and she cut through. Diffused light in the eastern sky signaled the beginning of the sunrise. Megan waded through the tall unkempt grass of a deserted farm. Behind the farmhouse was a potato cellar. Megan pulled open the door, and she dropped down inside. She let the door slam down behind her. *Right. Make a lot of noise.* She was angry at herself, but she was tired. The air felt warmer than outside, but it was stagnant. Megan coughed.

She felt around and found a flashlight on the dirt floor. She snapped it on and set it down so she could see what she was doing.

She carefully lowered the backpack to the floor. *Too heavy, maybe, for a couple of disassembled AR-18s.* As always, she resisted any desire to take a look at what was inside.

There was a gym bag she had left for herself on the floor. Megan quickly changed into a white blouse, thin gray sweater, and dark skirt. She changed to another pair of wool socks that reached almost up to her knees. Then she added a pair of good leather walking shoes. She straightened up to let down and comb her long dark hair.

The flashlight dimmed. She thought of her boyfriend. *Gotta tell Brian to pinch me some new batteries.*

Megan packed her running clothes in the gym bag and slung on the backpack again. She pushed open the cellar door and climbed out into the overgrown yard. The sky had brightened into the first gray of dawn. Back across the fields, she could see the mist on the hills she had just run through in the dark.

Megan rounded the house and followed the path she had mashed down on her way in through the tall grass. It was easier for her to keep her work clothes good as they could be. Back at the opening in the hedge, she dropped the backpack and hid it on the field side. Then she stepped out on the road holding her gym bag. There was a slight fog on the road as well as the mist in the trees.

Megan looked at her watch. It was a stylish Swiss-made watch. She had bought it with the money she made running the backpacks over the border. Brian had told her it was not a proper watch for a rebel to wear.

*I'm on time. I suppose your excuse'll be that your old Irish watch doesn't keep very good time.*

As if in answer, two headlights appeared in the fog down the road.

Megan tensed. The lights approached. Then she recognized the outline of Brian's dark pickup truck. Megan smiled and relaxed.

The truck pulled up alongside her and stopped. Megan retrieved the backpack from the other side of the hedge, and she followed that and her gym bag into the passenger side of the cab.

The young man behind the wheel leaned over and

let her give him a quick kiss.

He had shaggy brown hair, and he wore a dark green sweater and black jeans.

Megan adjusted the backpack on the floor to give herself more leg room, and held the gym bag on her lap.

The truck started forward. Megan folded her arms on top of the bag and leaned a little forward to better catch the warmth from the heat vent on the dash.

Brian drove carefully, keeping all the rules of the road. "That's an important package you brought over this morning," he said.

"It's cold. I'm chilled to the bone."

"I got a call," Brian said. "The big man himself wants to see you, don't ya know."

"What?" Megan asked.

"Hugh McConnell himself. He called during the night."

"Why's he want to see me?" Megan asked. She felt herself shiver despite the heated truck being much warmer than outside.

Brian gave a shrug. "I'd like to know too."

"What if I don't want to see him?" Megan asked.

Brian took his eyes off the road long enough to look over and give her a hard glare.

"Of course, I'll see him," Megan said quickly. *Don't tell me again about how we can never say no.* Then she added, "It's the 1970s now. Those old men like him are still fighting the Easter Rising of 1916."

"They are our leaders," he said. "It's fixed for tonight. I'll pick you up after school."

Megan gave a sigh and leaned back in her seat. She looked out the side window away from Brian. She had nothing more to say.

## Chapter Three

Megan went directly to the teacher's lounge after Brian dropped her off in front of the school. The room was warm, but its décor made it gloomy as the root cellar where she had changed clothes. It was used by the lay teachers in the Catholic school. The nuns had a room of their own.

Her friend Kate looked around after Megan came in the door. "Tired again," Kate said. "Don't you look like you were up all night again after seein' the ghost of Lawrence O'Connor."

Megan set down her gym bag and walked over to the heater. "I didn't see the ghost of Lawrence O'Connor," she said.

Kate's face formed into a knowing smile. "You were up all night with that Brian Branigan, then. I saw you get out of his truck." She gestured to the big front windows that let the teachers see all the activity on the street outside.

Megan spun around. She was upset, but she spoke calmly to her friend. "I'm cold because I was waiting outside for him to pick me up and give me a ride in this morning."

"Have a good hot tea, then," Kate said. She went over to the teapot and poured Megan a mug.

Megan relaxed. "Thanks."

"There's a new picture playin'," Kate said. "I

thought you might like to go with me, so I called."

"I got in real late," Megan lied.

"Your mother thought you were out with that Brian Branigan for the night."

Megan looked up over her mug and frowned. "My mother thinks a lot of things."

Kate glanced quickly around the room. None of the other teachers seemed close enough to overhear. Still, she lowered her voice to a confidential tone. "Your mother's very worried about you seeing him so much." She lowered her voice even more. "Everybody knows he's tied up with...some frightening people."

"I didn't spend the night with him," Megan said. She was thinking, *It's not a lie.* "He picked me up this morning and gave me a ride." *What guys do we know worth anything who don't have those kinds of connections?*

Kate looked at her and smiled. "Your mother told me she's afraid she'll have to start praying to Saint Gerard Majella for you."

"Right." Megan laughed. "Saint Gerard Majella, the patron saint of expectant mothers."

"That's the one." Kate nodded.

Megan was serious again. "Worry about yourself. Don't worry on that front about me."

Kate laughed. "If only I had a reason to. All the guys I know are either nerds or rebels. The decent ones don't seem to come my way."

Megan looked at her watch and made a face that said they both had better be aware of the time. Kate moved over to a table and set her mug down next to a pile of papers that she started to organize. Next to her papers was the morning newspaper. Megan could read the headline from where she stood. "Witnesses provide description of bus station bomber," it read. Under it was an artist's sketch of a young man. It looked like no one that Megan recognized.

Kate sensed Megan was looking at the paper. She pointed to the sketch. "Don't think I'll be surprised if Brian Branigan's face isn't in the paper like that some day."

"He's never said a word about that kind of thing being part of his life," Megan lied.

Kate let the answer go. "You want to go to the pictures with me tonight, then?"

"Sure, Megan said. Then she remembered. "Wait, no. I just remembered I made plans for tonight."

"How sure a bet would I be makin'," Kate asked, "if I bet you Brian Branigan was picking you up after school?"

"That's not something I'll bet on," Megan answered.

Kate spoke again in her quiet tone. "Just be careful," she warned. "I don't have to be a history teacher to know we haven't come all that far from the days when the British lined the sides of all the bridges with pikes holdin' up the captured rebels' rotting heads."

Megan gave her a wry smile. "Perhaps I can use that as the legend I teach the children today."

"No," Kate said. "You're the one who teaches the children about our legends and the stories of the fairies. I teach them the real things that happened, and don't start telling me the fairy stories are so much more fun."

"I was gonna tell 'em the story of Saint Bridget an' the cow," Megan said, "but maybe I'll do the one about the woman who caught a fairy. Then she turned her head for just a second, and the fairy was gone like he were made o' the same as the smoke and mists on the hills in the morning." Megan looked away out the front window, and she wished for just a second that when she looked back the teacher's room would have dissolved into the mists and fog of daybreak she had run through such a short time before. She looked back. Everything was the same.

Kate glanced quickly up at the clock on the wall. "I've got a parent to meet before school starts. I'll see if that picture is still playin' tomorrow."

"Good," Megan agreed.

Kate left. Megan sat down in the nearest chair. She exhaled heavily, and she finished her tea.

## Chapter Four

Megan left by the front door when the school day was over, carrying her gym bag as if it were full of weights. She caught sight of Brian's truck parked by the curb, and she let out a tired sigh.

"We have to drive to Belfast," Brian said. He had no words of greeting. "He wants to see you soon as he can."

Megan shrugged. She climbed into the truck and flopped down in the seat.

"I slept most of Sunday, but I get tired," Megan said. "Working with kids all day, and staying up half the night…"

Brian moved the truck forward. "You can sleep on the way."

Megan asked, "If he wants to see me so bad, why can't Hugh O'Connell bring his scrawny old ass here to Armaugh?"

"Hugh *Mc*Connell," Brian corrected her. "I'll be waitin' for you at Brady's Pub. We can have a pint or two there together before we head home."

"That place is always full of drunk rebel sympathizers," Megan complained. "Maybe someday you'll take me to a really nice place."

"Someday," Brian said, "maybe the Protestants'll give us some of the good jobs."

Megan sank down in her seat and drifted off to

sleep. When she woke, darkness had fallen, and they were on a crowded Belfast street.

Megan's eyes opened quickly, and she looked all around.

"Bloody Prods cloggin' up the road," Brian complained.

He turned a corner and pulled into an empty lot. Several cars were parked there. Two men sat in one of them.

"There they are," Brian said. He pointed to the two men in the car. "This must really be important. Those are two of his best men."

"Best men?" Megan asked.

"Go quickly. Get in the seat behind them."

Megan looked warily at the men. She did not move.

"Go quickly," Brian urged. He glanced around. "I'll be waitin' at the pub. I can't stay here long."

Megan gave a sigh. She got out of the truck and walked to the car.

The two men watched as she approached. The driver gestured toward the back seat with his head.

Megan got in and closed the door. She felt cramped in the back seat. The car smelled like stale cigarette smoke and beer.

The driver started the engine, and they moved quickly out into the crowded street. Brian had already pulled away.

The man in the passenger seat turned around. He handed Megan a balled-up piece of cloth. "Put this on, and keep your head down," he ordered.

Megan frowned. She spread the cloth out on her knee. "What is this?" she asked.

"Balaclava," the man answered.

"Oh, sure," Megan said. She recognized the traditional hood worn by the IRA to conceal their identity. She had never worn one for the jobs she did. She held it up to her face. It smelled of the sweat of many scared men.

"It'll mess my hair."

"Got some fight in her," the driver said. "And pretty too."

The other man looked around again. His unemotional eyes met her hard glare. "Eyeholes to the rear, dear. We'll find you a comb."

The driver glanced at her reflection in his mirror. "Both o' us would much rather keep lookin' at a pretty face like yours, but our commander is a marked man. It's best that you don't know where he stays."

Megan glanced out the window. "I live in Armaugh," she said. "I have no idea where I am right now."

"Security," the other man said with a shrug.

Jumping out and running didn't seem an appealing option. Megan took a big gulp of air and pulled the hood over her head.

"Now keep your head down," the man next to the driver ordered.

Megan obeyed. The position made her feel more cramped than before.

The car made a number of turns, and they rode for what seemed like a long time.

Megan considered trying to engage the two men in conversation. *You should come to Armaugh sometime,* she thought of saying. *Once it was the ecclesiastical capital of Ireland. Both religions have cathedrals there.*

*Before that, nearby Navan Fort was one of the great royal capitals of pagan Ireland...* But she kept quiet. She needed to focus on breathing in the hood.

The car finally stopped. Megan heard one of the men get out, and the door next to her opened.

"Go quickly," the voice of the driver came from the front seat.

Megan reached out.

A rough hand took hers, and she got out of the car. The hand pulled her quickly along. Megan stumbled up a pair of steps. Then she felt she was inside. It was warm, and the smell of boiling cabbage and potatoes penetrated the hood.

"Okay, dearie," the man's voice said from behind her. "You can pull that thing off now."

Megan quickly yanked the hood off her head. She shook her hair and took a big gulp of air. The light in the room was dim, but she could tell she was in the front room of a very small house. She was sure it was one of the many tenements found in the bigger towns, actually quite similar to the house she lived in with her mother in Armaugh. The smell of the food was stronger without the hood. Megan realized how hungry she was.

A sixtyish woman faced her from a dark doorway that undoubtedly led to the kitchen. The door behind her closed, and Megan realized that the man from the car had gone.

Megan tossed the balaclava into a nearby chair. "I'll quit if I have to keep wearin' these," she said.

The old woman waved her hand quickly in a gesture that dismissed the idea. "They shoot your kneecaps off for that," she said.

"What?" Megan said. She was shocked by the

woman's simple acceptance of the fact.

The woman stepped forward and bent down.

Megan instinctively stepped back. She realized there was a trap door in front of her feet.

The old woman lifted the door. "He's waitin' down there for you," she said.

Megan could see a ladder in the semi-darkness below. She wished very much she were wearing her running clothes rather than the skirt and hard shoes she had worn for school.

Megan turned around and stepped down carefully on the top rung. It was solid, and she went on down. As she descended, her eyes adjusted better to the light. She saw crates in front of her. They were stacked almost to the underside of the floor above. Her feet reached the dirt floor. Megan spun around and looked in the opposite direction.

An old man sat behind a door that had been laid over two barrels to make a desk. Megan was surprised. She had expected the revered Hugh McConnell to be a much more imposing figure than the bent, gray-haired man who faced her from across the horizontal door. A lantern burned on a barrel behind him. His exact features were obscured by the way the light shone.

Megan spoke first. "I've been told you sent for me."

She could see that a slight smile formed on his lips. "They told me that you have a bit of spirit."

Megan was again surprised. His voice was powerful. In that way he was very imposing.

"They've also told me you've been crossin' the border for us."

"I have." Megan nodded. "More than a few times."

"They tell me you're very good at it."

Megan remained impassive.

"I knew your uncle," he said, "and your father, but him not too well."

"I didn't know that." Megan was surprised.

"They were both good fighters. They served the cause well."

"My father never spoke of it," Megan said.

"We wouldn't have asked you to help us if we hadn't known your family," the old man said.

Megan had a sudden chill. She wondered what else they might know.

"I miss them," McConnell said. Then he laughed. "I miss all the old guard. I've outlived them all."

Megan didn't understand his humor.

He became serious. "I heard you came over the border last night," he said.

"The fog was cold this morning," Megan said. "I think my bones still have the chill."

A broad smile crossed the old man's face. "I'm sure you're quite a sight when you appear out of the mists on the hills."

Megan gave him a wary look.

"They tell me you teach our old legends to the children," McConnell said. "Do we have one about the mists on the hills?"

"I've lots of stories about the fairies, and lots of them have mists," Megan said, "but the Brits have the big mists story, the one about King Arthur coming back through the mists of Avalon to make England supreme again."

McConnell frowned. "You think England will rise again, then?" he asked.

"No." Megan laughed. "I haven't seen a Brit yet that wasn't fumblin' around in a fog."

McConnell laughed too, and Megan felt more at ease.

Then he was serious again. "There's someone I want you to lead through our mists on the border," he said. "One of my boys got in a little trouble, and we're sending him south, where he can be safe for a while."

"No," Megan said quickly. "I've never taken anyone over the border before. I always run alone. I need to be free to react if there's trouble."

"Don't think of him as a person," McConnell said. "He'll just be like a cargo, really, like those backpacks you bring north. Except this one walks on its own."

"What if he makes noise?" Megan asked.

"Boy's name is Mick," McConnell said. He gave a sigh. "Same age as you, but he's shown us he's still got the mind o' a child."

Megan gave her wary look again.

"Normally we'd just point the way and send him over on his own," McConnell said. "But we especially don't want him gettin' stopped, ya see. This cargo needs a bit o' helpin' hand."

"My hand?" Megan said.

McConnell looked straight at her. "You're the one."

Megan felt a chill, but she knew well enough that she couldn't really refuse. "You're going to make sure he knows not to make noise on me?" she asked.

"He'll know. You can count on that," McConnell assured her. "He's smart enough to appreciate the spot he's got himself in. Smart enough to keep his mouth shut and do what we and you say."

Megan let that fact sink in.

"He's related to a recent hero," the old man continued, "the famous freedom fighter Phineus McGuire, from the Belfast riots of '68. Challenged one of the Brits because he thought they had the usual rubber bullets in their guns. Didn't realize he was up against a proud Highland regiment that had just arrived to stop all the troubles we were causin'. They hadn't gotten the word on the policy with the bullets. We all learned a lesson from his mistake."

Megan thought, *And for that, you made him a hero?* But she held her tongue.

"He really shouldn't be any trouble to you at all. He's far from *duine le dia,*" McConnell said, using the Gaelic for simpleminded or an idiot. "We just don't trust his ability to get over on his own."

"If he does the least thing stupid, he'll find himself on his own," Megan warned.

"He'll be told not to be stupid," McConnell said in a way that sent another chill down Megan's spine. Then, just as quickly, the warm smile returned to the old man's face. "I like your spirit," he said. "You certainly are doing your family proud."

"Thanks," Megan said.

"Your friend Brian will pick you up next weekend as usual," McConnell said. "He'll have your cargo. You just get him...it...to the farm where you always go on the other side. Someone else will take him from there."

Footsteps sounded overhead. They both looked quickly up.

"Ah, the car has come back for you," McConnell said. He extended his hand across the door that served as his desk. "Godspeed, and God save Ireland."

"Yes, God save Ireland," Megan echoed as she shook the strong old hand.

"We must talk about all the old legends sometime," McConnell said. "But go quickly. The car can't wait here long."

Megan nodded. She turned and climbed the ladder. The trap door opened above her as she did.

The old woman handed Megan a balaclava after she had climbed out of the cellar. "Here's a fresh one I laundered just yesterday, and here's a comb for when you're done."

"Thanks," Megan said with genuine appreciation.

"I do what I can to take care of our men," the old woman said. The woman gave a knowing look that made Megan realize that she herself was now one of the old woman's "men" too.

"Now put that on. We must hurry," a voice said from behind her. The man from the car had been standing by the front door.

Megan complied and held out her hand. Again she was led across the sidewalk and helped into the back seat of a car. The men in the front were silent as they drove along. Megan had no desire to start a conversation.

The car stopped, and one of the men suddenly said, "You can take that thing off now."

Megan ripped the balaclava off her head and threw it on the car floor. She saw she was on the fairly lit and busy street in front of Brady's Pub.

"Get out and walk in there like you was goin' to meet your friends," the driver said. "Don't go callin' any attention to us, now."

"Okay," Megan agreed.

"Maybe even wave us goodbye," the driver added. "Like maybe we were friends who gave you a ride."

"Right," Megan said. "Thanks for the ride."

"Our pleasure, dear," the driver said.

The other man echoed, "Our pleasure, indeed."

Megan got out of the car, sort of waved, and walked deliberately through the door into Brady's Pub.

The bar had a fairly good crowd for a weekday night. Megan knew that because a lot of unemployed Catholics gathered there. She spotted Brian sitting alone at the bar. Megan crossed through the tables to him. There was a singer with a guitar on a little stage at the rear. He had just finished a rousing rendition of a rebel song. The patrons applauded enthusiastically. "God bless Ireland!" someone shouted, and the singer launched into another song.

"I'll order a pint for you," Brian said. "You can tell me how it went on the way home."

"No," Megan said. "I mean, no to the pint. I'm exhausted. I'm going to the loo and comb out my hair. Then we're going home."

Brian looked displeased.

"How many pints have you had?" Megan asked.

"No more than usual." Brian shrugged.

"Maybe I should do the driving," Megan said, and she left him at the bar.

Megan didn't fight Brian when they got in his truck and he took the wheel. "So how'd it go?" he asked as soon as they started down the street.

"Whole thing was right out of a bad movie," Megan complained. "Only thing missing was a table full of old men puttin' down pints and shots an' singin' the same damn songs they sing in that pub. They made me wear a bloody balaclava backwards so I couldn't see where they were going."

"That's strong words," Brian said.

"Then Hugh O'Connell meets me in a dirty, dark cellar," Megan continued.

"Hugh *Mc*Connell," Brian corrected her again. "I've never seen him. What did he want with you?"

"I've been appointed to take some loser south across the border with me on my next run," Megan said. "He's a fool, so someone has to show him the way. That's all there is to it. I don't see why it's such a big deal. I don't want to do it. I like to run it alone. But I know I have to take him."

"It all was so urgent." It was obvious to her that Brian didn't really know what was going on.

"They'll send word to take me down to the border Friday night, I'm sure, even though I don't usually go two weekends in a row."

"It's all something special, I suppose." Brian shrugged.

They fell into silence as the houses passed by. Megan noticed that a couple of them had been burned out. She wondered if that was from the rioting. There were British soldiers on some of the corners. They didn't seem interested in Brian's truck that night. Megan slouched back and drifted off into a restless sleep while he drove on.

Chapter Five

The next night, Megan arrived home right after school was over. Her mother looked surprised when she walked in the door. The older woman looked like a gray-haired copy of her daughter except for the vitality that was no longer there.

"You came straight home from school?" her mother asked.

"I'm going to the pictures later with my friend Kate," Megan said. She stood just inside the front door. The front room of the little house that Megan had grown up in felt warm compared to the damp early evening air, even though it was hardly bigger than the front room of the Belfast tenement Megan had been in the night before.

"That Brian Branigan gave you a ride home again," her mother said. "I know the sound o' that truck of his."

The mother put down the book she had been reading. "I know how you can give me a whole learned lecture about how you're an adult now, and I can no longer put you in the care of the good nuns of Saint Patrick. But I know you go off every weekend with that boyfriend of yours, and I know, for sure, it's not for any good."

Megan let out a long sigh and resisted the wish to sit down. "Mother, I've said all this before. I might not make good enough money to have a place of my own yet, but I'm not going to spend all my free time sittin' around here. I love running through the countryside. I feel really happy when I run. It's like I go into the world of the fairies and such, like I can go to a place where everything is like I want it to be. I have lots of friends here and there, and they usually let me stay over. I do not spend all my time with Brian Branigan."

"Father O'Leary is even wonderin' why you're so often not with me in church on Sundays anymore. So many o' you young people seem t' have lost your faith. It's a wonder t' me the nuns hired you at their school."

"And," Megan said, "don't go telling me again how I'm gonna have to start prayin' to Saint What's-his-name, the patron of knocked-up women. That's not going to happen to me."

Her mother started to cry. Megan made no move to comfort her. "I just worry about you," her mother said. "I care what happens. I just sit here and wonder all the time you're gone."

Megan sighed again and sat down in the chair nearest her mother. "I know what I'm doing," she tried to assure her mother. "I'll be fine."

"I mostly worry about what people say that Brian Branigan is involved in," her mother said. She pointed to a pile of papers and magazines by her chair. The paper with the artist sketch of the bomber sat atop the pile. "One o' these days it might be Brian Branigan they're drawin' about," she said.

"Aren't most of the men of our religion involved in some way with those kinds of things?" Megan asked. She remembered what Hugh McConnell had said about her relatives. That had been news to her. "What about my father? Didn't he go off with his friends a lot? What about his brother?"

"If your father ever had anything to do with them, he never told me," her mother said. It was such a strong statement Megan felt it must have been true that her mother didn't know.

"He and his brother both had good jobs at that good Catholic tractor business their uncle owned," her mother added. "They both went off a lot for their work. They sold tractors to the farmers all over the north."

"So you didn't worry the same when he stayed out late?" Megan asked.

"Not the same way I worry about what might happen if you're with that Brian Branigan," her mother said. "When his friends came and said your father had died of a heart attack on a business trip, it was a total shock to me."

"Right," Megan agreed. She started to ask, "Didn't that seem a little odd?" But Megan kept quiet. She thought it best her mother not know what Hugh McConnell had said.

Her mother spoke up again. "That's why I was so glad when you were born that you were a girl. I knew I wouldn't have to worry about you getting into the kind of trouble so many of the boys get into."

Megan almost said, "Times have changed, mother dear." But instead she stood up and said, "I'd best get changed now. Kate'll be coming round soon with her car."

## Chapter Six

When Megan came out of school on Friday, Brian was there. She had brought her gym bag with her running clothes and shoes. She was surprised to see that the usually empty back of Brian's truck was filled with what looked like roofing material.

"What's up?" Megan asked as he opened the passenger side door. "You get a job fixin' somebody's roof?"

"I wish," Brian said. "Get in, and I'll tell you."

Megan climbed into the truck.

Brian started the engine and pulled quickly away. "It's him!" he said. "No wonder Hugh McConnell wanted to see you personally."

"Him?" Megan asked.

"The one they got drawin's of all over the papers and on the telly. I got him hidden under that tarp in the middle. I get stopped, we're dead."

"Him!" Megan said again. "You mean it's the one who bombed the bus station?"

Brian didn't have to answer. She could see how he was concentrating on the road, and how tight his grip was on the wheel.

"Hugh McConnell never told me it was him I'd be takin' across," Megan said.

"They told me to load up all that shit back there," Brian said. "And they told me to leave a space down the middle. Then he just comes walkin' up and says, 'I'm the one.' I recognized him right away. I damn near shit my pants right there."

"He better not do anything dumb," Megan said. "That old man shoulda told me I'd be escortin' Northern Ireland's most wanted man."

"God, be careful. I've been sweatin' ever since I got him."

"I hope he's rested up plenty, for a good fast run," Megan said. "Does he have on dark clothes?"

"Yeah, pretty much," Brian said. "I'd a thought the old man would've told you who he was."

"Said his name was Mick," Megan said. "Son of... I think he said Phineus McGuire."

"I've seen him before," Brian said, "but I didn't know who he was. That's their method. Give 'em to a different section. Keep 'em away from their friends when they're number one wanted."

Brian carefully turned a corner where a policeman was standing. After they were safely past, he let out a long breath. "I better fix somebody's roof before I drive past that corner again," he said.

"I don't suppose we could just drop him off somewhere and point him toward the border?" Megan asked.

"Now you're goin' balmy on me!"

"Sorry," Megan said quickly. "I didn't mean to be makin' fun."

"Right. Don't go scarin' me with those kinds o' thoughts," Brian said. "I'm close enough to a heart attack with him just bein' in the back."

Megan put a hand on his arm. "It'll be startin' to get dark by the time we get to the border," she said.

"I'll get him over quick as I can."

"I'll be back for you as usual, day after tomorrow," Brian said.

"It'll be Sunday this time," Megan said. "I won't have to get to school in the mornin'. I can sleep the rest o' Sunday, if I want to."

"I won't be doin' much sleepin' myself till I know you're back safe."

They were on a straight, uncrowded stretch of road. Megan leaned over and gave him a quick kiss on the cheek.

Brian took his attention off the road long enough to flash her a quick smile.

## Chapter Seven

Megan left Mick under the back porch of the deserted farmhouse while she went into the potato cellar and changed into her running clothes. His actual resemblance to the drawing in the paper was frightening. Someone had remembered his features very well.

When Megan got back to him, it was just about time to start their journey.

Mick sat rubbing his knees. "Bloody long ride in that truck," he said. "That friend o' yours wouldn't even let me out to take a pee."

"Take one now if you have to," Megan said, "'cause I'm not gonna let you stop for one either."

"I took one while you were gone," Mick said.

Megan looked up to gauge the darkness of the sky. Then she looked back at him. "You keep right behind me," she instructed. "Don't go wanderin' off, and don't take any notions you can do anything on your own."

Mick glared at her. "You like actin' tough, don't you," he said.

Megan gave him her wry smile. "You're lucky that friend of mine didn't stash you in some dustbin till dark," she said. "Hugh McConnell himself promised me you wouldn't cause me any trouble."

The name seemed to carry some weight. Mick continued to glare, but he said no more.

Megan looked at the dark sky again. Just the slightest crescent of moon and some bright stars had appeared. She would have liked it to be a little darker, with perhaps just one star to wish on that this job was over and done.

"We're going along the road first," she said. "Keep real close to the hedge, and if I say, 'Get down!' do it fast. You understand me?"

Mick gave a sullen nod.

"Let's go," Megan said.

She led the way through the tall grass to the break in the hedge and out onto the side of the road. They walked along at a decent pace.

"It's cold," Mick complained.

Megan glanced back over her shoulder. "It's always cold at night here," she said. "And please, keep your trap shut unless you've got something important to say."

She could feel the look he gave her from behind.

Suddenly Megan stopped, and she stiffened.

"What?" Mick asked.

"Shut up," Megan snapped.

They heard a vehicle approaching.

"Get down," Megan said.

Mick obeyed her right away. They both flattened themselves against the ground at the bottom of the hedge.

The sound grew louder. One, two, maybe three trucks, Megan decided.

Headlights shone through the trees. They swung around a curve, and the lights passed quickly over the heads of Megan and Mick. After they passed, a backwash of diesel exhaust filled the air.

"Stay down," Megan said in Mick's direction in as loud a whisper as she dared.

A second truck passed and continued down the road, and then a third. That one stopped a bit down the road. It sat for a few moments. Then it went on.

"It's the Brits," Mick whispered after they had gone. There was fear in his voice. "They're droppin' off soldiers along the road."

"Shut up!" Megan snapped at him.

She listened for what seemed like a long time. "I don't hear anything more," she whispered. "I go across this way because they don't patrol here often."

"They're out lookin' for me everywhere," Mick said. Megan sensed he was trembling.

"Even if they're out here, they've gotta find us first," Megan whispered back. "Once we're in the south, we're safe. Are you comin' with me?"

"They say you know what you're doin'," Mick said, but what she could see of his face in the slight moonlight said he was not sure.

Megan got up. She wiped the dirt from the side of the road off her hands and onto the rear of her jeans. "Let's go," she said, and she started walking again, along the hedge. Mick got up and followed close behind.

"If we do meet somebody," Megan said softly back over her shoulder, "don't even pretend you can talk."

Megan reached another break in the hedge, and she headed through into some woods. Despite his reluctance, Mick was right behind her.

They walked on in silence for a while, through the trees. Megan felt the damp and cold. She was already anxious for the warm cup of tea that she knew her friend Colleen would make as soon as they arrived at the farmhouse on the other side.

Megan stopped. She moved close to Mick and whispered just loud enough for him to hear. "From here on we run," she said.

Megan made a quick mental wish to the fairies to protect her. Then she turned and started to run.

Megan could always find her way through the woods, and she knew well the direction to go. She heard Mick's breathing and his footsteps right behind her. The running made her feel warmer, but it felt very strange to have someone else along. She definitely did not feel good about this run.

"Hello?" a strange voice suddenly called out from the darkness.

Megan stopped short.

Mick slammed into her, and they both fell to the ground.

"Who goes there?" the voice demanded.

"Shit, it's the Brits," Megan whispered. "Don't move."

"Oh, God…" the boy whimpered.

"Over here," the voice called. "I think I heard something."

Searchlights snapped on, and the beams flashed all around over their heads.

"Over here," the voice called out. "I think I've got something." The accent was definitely British.

The lights all moved toward an area a little away from Megan and Mick.

There was a quick rustling, and the lights went toward the noise.

"I see it," a voice said. "Fox or somethin'."

"God-damned hedgehog, if you ask me," another voice said, and there was some laughter.

"I don't think that's what I heard," the original voice said. It was suddenly very quiet, and the soldiers were all serious again.

The lights flashed around over Megan's and Mick's heads again. Then the closest one turned in the opposite direction. Mick took it as an opportunity. He jumped up.

"Get down!" Megan ordered in the loudest whisper she dared.

Mick took off, running back the way they had come. To Megan, the noise he made was deafening. The lights all swung his way.

"Halt, or we shoot," one of the soldiers yelled.

Megan raised her head enough to see the lights flashing all around.

Then one of the soldiers fired the first warning shot in the air. Mick ran on. The lights found him. He stopped and turned to face their glare, and he raised his hands.

"Stand right there, and keep those hands up," a voice ordered.

Megan saw the lights moving to converge on Mick. She jumped up and ran south faster and more quietly than she had ever run before.

## Chapter Eight

Megan pounded desperately on Colleen's door. It opened just a crack, then quickly all the way.

"Jesus, Mary, and Joseph, you're in a state," Colleen said. "What happened to you?"

Megan stumbled into the room and sat quickly in the nearest wooden chair. She was taking deep breaths. She looked at her hands. They were trembling.

"You must've seen a banshee or somethin'," Colleen said. "You must've had quite a fright." Then Colleen realized something. "Where's that boy you were supposed t' be bringin' along?"

"Caught," Megan managed to say. She was better catching her breath. "Brits got 'im. They almost got me."

"Oh, God..." Colleen said.

"There were patrols out tonight," Megan said. "They were hidin' in the woods, keepin' quiet. We ran right by one."

"Thank God you got away," Colleen said. "Did they get a look at you?"

"No," Megan said. "This stupid boy they give me... We're on the ground doin' good... Then the lights go the other way. He jumps up and starts to run."

"What a fool," Colleen agreed.

"They fired a shot, an' they got their lights on him," Megan said. "He gave up, an' they got 'im."

"Wow," Colleen said. "Do you think he'll talk? Do you think he'll tell 'em about you?"

"I hope not," Megan said. "They all went after him, so I got away. I don't think any of the Brits saw me. If he doesn't tell 'em, I don't think they'll know I was even there."

"God, you are so lucky."

"I know what I'm doing," Megan corrected her. "Why did they give me such a fool?"

Colleen let out a long breath. Then she went into action. "Sit tight," she said. "I'll have to call an' tell 'em not to send the man who was going to take him away. But first I'll put on some tea."

"Good," Megan said. "Since I started the run, I've been wantin' some o' your tea."

Megan sat almost without any thoughts as she waited for the tea. Slowly, her mind calmed, and she started to process what she had just been through. As her mind cleared, she said a silent "thank you" to her fairies, who she felt had heard and protected her.

"God, I'm really frightened now," Megan said after Colleen brought her a cup of strong, warm tea. "Sometimes when I run through the woods near the old mounds where the fairies are said t' be, I imagine the fairies all around me. I imagine a world full of magical fairies helpin' me run along. I ask 'em t' protect me all the time. But not tonight. The soldiers were real. They seemed all around us too. They had real guns. They woulda killed me in a instant. Then that damn Hugh McConnell woulda made me one o' their heroes."

"They might've just captured you," Colleen said, "like they did the boy."

"Likely that'd be worse," Megan said. "Either way

my mother'd die. The shock of knowin' what I'm really doin' would do her in."

"I don't know." Colleen didn't agree. "Don't the rebels say their women that stay at home are sometimes tougher'n them?"

Megan ignored the question. "Now when I run I'm going to see soldiers instead o' fairies," she said. "It'll never be the same."

"Hope you're not in trouble with our people now, too," Colleen said.

"In trouble?" Megan was surprised by the question. "He ran like a coward. I kept tellin' him to keep down. Hugh McConnell himself said he was a fool. In fact Hugh McConnell can take a flyin' leap for givin' 'im to me."

"Now, that's pretty strong," Colleen said. "So, you think you're safe with this McConnell leader, then?"

"He told me the boy was a fool," Megan said again.

"My brother's the one who arranges for people to get away an' start a new life," Colleen said. "He does it really discreet, whether it's the Brits or the IRA you're in trouble with. He doesn't let the wrong people know a thing. He'd sure do it for you, if I asked 'im to."

"No, I've got a job," Megan disagreed. "I'm a teacher. I've got a decent career among many who don't have one. I know how lucky I am."

"I don't dispute that," Colleen said. "But if you find y' are in trouble with them, my offer'll stand."

"Thanks, but I don't think I'll have t' collect on something like that," Megan said.

"I live in the south," Colleen continued. "The Brits can't get me, or you, here, but if you've crossed the

IRA, that doesn't matter a bit. The only thing you can do is start a new life somewhere far away, like in America or Australia."

"No," Megan said. "As long as that fool doesn't break the code and rat on me, I'll be fine. Then I'll see about maybe movin' south, but not far away like America."

"Suit yourself." Colleen shrugged. "Here, you've finished that cup already. You must still be feelin' the cold. Let me get you some more tea."

"Thanks," Megan said again. "My fairies'll protect me against Hugh McConnell like they did against the Brits. I'm not worried about him."

Colleen had stood to get the tea, but she stopped and looked back at Megan. "Ya know, I don't think you have any idea what you've got yourself involved in," she said.

Megan thought a moment before she answered. "It's true," she admitted. "I didn't even realize how much I've become one o' them till they took me to see Hugh McConnell. But now I've seen him, I trust him to understand how stupid that boy was."

Colleen went and got another cup of tea without comment. She brought it back and sat down opposite.

Megan took a long, slow sip. Then she said, "I started all this as a lark, ya know. When we were kids, I liked t' throw bottles at the Brits just like the boys. Sure, I've been to a rebel funeral or two, but I never thought I was doin' anything to make me really one of them. I mean, I love to run. I've been Brian Branigan's girlfriend since we were kids. We'd go around a corner an' both throw a bottle over a wall at a policeman or somethin'. Then we'd run like hell together. I always thought I should be able t' do anything the boys did. I'll admit, runnin' missions for 'em is a lark for me, just like throwin' bottles at the soldiers."

"You're not a little girl any more," Colleen said. "Ya just told me how scared you were that those soldiers' guns were real. Maybe it's time t' stop playin' kid's games."

Megan shrugged. "I will tell 'im when I get back," she said, "that I'm not takin' anyone along with me again."

Colleen let the statement hang and changed the subject. "It's late. You've had a real fright. You better get some rest. Maybe I better give you some whiskey in another cup o' tea."

"Yes, I'll have some whiskey, thanks," Megan said. "Then I'll try to sleep." After a moment, she added, almost as if she were trying to reassure herself, "The Brits got their man. They're not gonna care a tuppence for me. And the IRA knows he's a right fool. I'll be fine."

Colleen said, "Ya know, next t' rebel songs, the ones we sing the most are of leavin' Ireland." She held up her hand to stop Megan from arguing. Colleen then went to the sideboard and got the bottle of her best whiskey for Megan.

## Chapter Nine

Megan made it back across the border on her own well before daylight. The effect of the whiskey and lack of sleep was balanced by increased adrenaline. Patty had brought her a backpack like usual, but this one was lighter than the last. She had prayed to her fairies as soon as she set out. She studied the stars and the sliver of a moon overhead, and she made sure to make a wide diversion around the area where Mick had been captured the night before. It was near the mound where she always felt the presence of her protecting fairies. The mounds were old forts built by an earlier civilization to defend their land. As she ran, Megan thought of the story she told the children of the woman who captured the fairy, then lost him when she looked away. *Why couldn't I have looked away from Hugh McConnell, and he would have disappeared into the dampness of his dark cellar?*

She waited a while in the potato cellar, not wanting to wait by the side of the road any longer than she had to. It was Sunday, so she didn't have to change for school. She knew the word would be out right away. She hoped Brian would come as usual. Colleen was the only one who could contact anyone when she was across the border. Calling Brian was not an option

Megan looked at her watch. She took a deep breath and emerged from the cellar. The fog had come in and brought with it an ominous gray sky. *Thank God last night was clear,* she thought, *and I had the stars to guide me.*

She walked quickly and got to their meeting place by the side of the road.

Megan did her best not to pace, though she felt the urge to keep moving. The fog lifted a little, and the sky brightened just a little, as well. She saw the familiar outline of Brian's truck coming down the road, and she breathed a sigh of relief. She picked up her gym bag and retrieved the backpack she had brought.

Brian stopped quickly. He leaned over and flung open the door for her. "Thank the Lord above you're all right," he said.

Megan climbed in. They hugged awkwardly, leaning over the gearshift and the space between the seats.

"They didn't say anything on the news about there bein' anybody but the bomber," Brian said. "We were on pins an' needles till we got the call from the farm that you were there." He pulled away and headed for Armaugh.

"No artist sketch o' me in the papers, then?" Megan asked.

"No, none o' that," Brian assured her.

That news made Megan feel a lot better. She gave Brian a recounting of the event similar to the one she had given Colleen after she arrived at the farmhouse.

"We figured it was all his fault," Brian said. "He's disgraced the name of his father, Phineaus McGuire, as well. He is such a fool."

"Fool enough t' tell 'em about me?" Megan asked.

"I don't think so," Brian said.

That made Megan feel better.

"If he had," Brian added, "they woulda had a sketch o' you in the papers and on the telly this morning. Let's hope they don't break his commitment t' the cause so's he breaks our code o' silence. But I don't think even a fool would do that."

Megan sat back in her seat and tried to relax. She wanted to tell Brian about how stupid she was starting to think this all was, but something told her to hold her tongue. Something told her she should discuss it with her fairies before she risked upsetting anything. They passed along the road and into the first few houses of Armaugh. "Where are we headed?" she asked.

"It's Sunday. There's no school today," Brian said. "I thought we'd stop at the pub an' both calm down over a pint or two."

"No," Megan said. "I'm exhausted. Drop me home. I want to sleep the rest o' the day away."

Brian made a face showing his displeasure, but he knew better than to disagree. "If ya please," he said.

"Thanks," Megan said. She wanted to add that the last thing she wanted was to be in a bar full of freedom fighters, listening to their damn rebel songs right then, or even their sad songs of leaving Ireland, but she kept quiet.

Brian pulled up in front of her house. Megan gave him a quick kiss over the space between them. "Have a pint for me," she said. Then she opened the door and hopped down from the truck. She crossed the sidewalk and got into the house without looking back.

Thankfully, her mother wasn't in the front room when Megan went in. The older woman was off to church on a Sunday morning, for sure. There was the morning paper on top of a pile by her mother's chair. Megan didn't even have to pick it up to see what she was looking for. "Captured bomber refuses to talk," the headline read. There was a police mug shot of Mick on the front page, as well.

"The fool," Megan said out loud. She shook her head and went on upstairs to her room.

## Chapter Ten

"Don't you look the proper wreck this mornin'," Kate said when Megan entered the teacher's room the next day.

"I didn't sleep very well," Megan said. Then she added quickly, "But I did sleep at home alone."

"Me thinks thee doth protest too much."

Megan decided the best response to Kate's Shakespeare reference was laughter.

"I'd better make you a tea right away," Kate said.

Megan flopped down in one of the ancient stuffed chairs. *Why has my life come to where everybody thinks they need to make me tea?*

Kate poured her a cup of very hot tea. Megan started to take a sip, then decided to let it cool.

"I'm sure you heard that man the Brits wanted for bombin' the bus station was caught tryin' t' cross the border," Kate said.

Megan felt a chill. She lifted her teacup so the steam warmed her face, and she could breathe it in.

"I hope that Brian Branigan o' yours didn't have anything t' do with that," Kate said.

"No, not him," Megan lied. She wondered what the reaction would be if she added, "It was Brian drove him an' me to the border, an' it was me that was tryin t' get 'im over, actually." But she didn't say that.

"How do you know he didn't?" Kate asked. "Those

kind are always so secret about everything."

Megan shrugged. "I just do."

"Although you were probably out with 'im when the Brits got their man," Kate said. "I tried to call you Saturday night. Your mother said you weren't home."

"I musta gotten in later," Megan lied.

"Why don't you get him to marry you?" Kate asked. "It'd save you a lot of wear 'n' tear."

Megan set her cup down, and she gave her friend a "What are you talking about?" look.

"Sorry, I didn't mean anything," Kate said quickly. "Look, I admit I'm a bit jealous—a lot, actually—of you havin' a boyfriend an' the fun you must be havin' with him."

Megan softened her look, and she picked up her tea.

"Just look at me," Kate said. "I'm so well rested all the time."

One of the other teachers put her head in the door. "Megan," she said. "Finian O'Farrell's grandfather is out here. He wants t' have a word with you."

Megan frowned. "With me?" she asked. She put her tea down again and pulled herself out of the chair. As always, she felt stiff from the long runs the two nights before. "O'Farrell is one of the best boys in his group," she said. "I gave him a good grade. What's he want with me?"

Kate shrugged. "Parents," she said. "An' grandparents are sometimes worse."

Megan went out into the hallway.

An old man in a tattered wool suit and an open overcoat stood waiting for her. The eyes looked bright, even devious, in contrast with his sallow skin and thinning white hair. He beckoned and drew her into a dark corner of the hallway.

"Pleased to meet you," he said in a voice she could barely hear.

His breath and clothes smelled heavily of cigarette smoke. She was sure he had certainly seen hard years during which he'd had too much beer, as well.

"Your grandson is doing very well in my story group," Megan said. "He pays attention all the time."

"Ah," the old man said. "That's so very good t' hear."

A brief trace of a proud smile crossed his face. Then he became serious again. He spoke with even less volume, and Megan had to lean closer to hear.

"I knew your father," he said. Then he gave her a wink.

Megan felt a sudden chill. "What do you mean?" she asked.

The old man quickly touched a finger to his lips. She was surprised by the speed of his hand.

"We're all proud o' you," he said softly again. "Your friend Brian made 'is report, an' I thought it was important that someone tell you that right away."

"Proud o' me?" Megan asked. She looked at him with a puzzled face.

"We don't want you thinkin' you're in any trouble for what happened on the border Friday night," he said.

Megan suddenly realized what the old man was talking about and who he meant by "we."

"We knew that boy was a fool," the old man continued. "Thank God you got away."

"I don't think they ever saw me," Megan said. "I stayed down and hidden. I stayed calm. That's all he woulda had t' do…" Megan's mind was racing. She was thinking this old man must have crawled out of the same damp cellar that Hugh McConnell hid in. She had always thought that schools were some kind of neutral territory. She desperately wanted to find a way to get rid of him.

"I just hope that fool won't say anything," Megan added.

"He won't," the old man said. There was something very cold and disturbing in the way he said it.

Then the old man's eyes softened, and his voice got even softer. "We've got big plans for you, ya know," he said. His eyes suddenly sparkled, and he gave her his wink again.

"Plans?" Megan asked in a voice that was probably way too loud. She whispered again, "What plans?"

A boney hand reached out and touched Megan's wrist. She recoiled. It was a reflex reaction.

"All in good time, my dear," the old man said. "When the time comes, you will see."

Megan had nothing to say.

The old man stepped away toward a brighter part of the hall. His voice rose so anyone near them could hear. "Yes, thank you, ma'am," he said. "Thank you again for that fine commendation of that grandson o' mine. Just like his grandfather, sharp as a whip. I'll be sure t' pass it on t' his parents when I see 'em tonight. They will be so proud o' him."

He turned and winked at Megan again. "An' you can be sure," he added, "that I'll come check on his progress again."

"Thank you," Megan managed, though she wanted

to say, "Please don't ever come in here again."

She folded her arms and remained standing where she was as the old man shuffled down the hallway away from her and turned to go out the front door. Her mind raced with more thoughts than she was able to put together. The door opened next to her, and Kate came out of the teacher's lounge. "What'd he want?" she asked.

"What?" Megan asked. Then her mind came back to school. "The old man? He just wanted t' say how proud he is o' all o' us," she lied. "It makes no sense that he came in."

"That was nice o' him," Kate said. "It's nice when they come here for somethin' other than t' complain."

"Yes," Megan agreed. Then she spoke the truth. "He didn't come t' complain."

Megan dropped her arms and took a deep breath. It was time to start the school day.

## Chapter Eleven

Brian was there again to pick up Megan at the end of the school day. When she went out the door, she found his truck parked at the curb. As she approached, Megan noticed the roofing material was gone from the back. She also realized she hadn't paid that any mind when he'd picked her up that morning. She still didn't feel a whole lot less upset. Brian pulled quickly away from the curb.

"Hugh McConnell wants t' see ya again," Brian said after Megan got in.

"Again?" Megan asked. "You don't even give me a hello. You're tellin' me we gotta go t' Belfast again? Wasn't it enough the old man came t' school an' told me everything is fine?"

"Old man?" Brian asked. He swerved slightly. Then he brought the truck back to its proper lane, and he looked over at her with a frown.

"O'Farrell's grandfather came into school," Megan said. "An' he drew me aside."

"O'Farrell?" Brian asked. The frown changed to surprise.

"Out o' nowhere, he starts talkin' t' me about Friday night," Megan said. "It was like he'd been invited along. Pulls me aside in the hallway o' the school, like I'm supposed t' even know who he is. Then he winks at me like he's a creepy old pervert or something…" Megan noticed Brian's expression. "What's wrong?" she asked.

"I'm supposed t' be your contact," Brian said. "I don't like them sendin' him t' talk to you instead o' me. I know this was a big job, real important to the cause an' all, but I don't like it. That's all."

"Well, that's what they did," Megan said. "Or maybe he did it on his own."

"No," Brian disagreed. ""Ya don't go talkin' t' people on your own."

"How should I know?" Megan said. "Nobody ever gave me the rule book t' read."

"There's no rule book," Brian said. "You pay attention, an' ya learn how things are done."

Megan set her mouth in an irritated pout. "An' suppose I don't care how things are done?" she asked.

"It's like when the nuns teach us about religion," Brian said. "It's just the way it is, that's all." Then he quickly added, "Besides, ya should relax. Ya don't need t' be worryin' about all this right now. You'll need t' be rested when we get t' Belfast."

Megan ignored him. "This creepy old man comes right into school today an' pulls me aside," she complained. "How am I supposed t' teach the children about Shan Van Vocht, the old woman who is Ireland, after some old man throws me off like that? I hate the way you all do everything that way, an' how everybody knows everything about you an' your family whether you told 'em anything or not."

"Not everybody knows everything," Brian said. "In fact, there's an awful lot that's only known by a few."

"Then he tells me they have plans for me," Megan said.

"Plans?" Brian was surprised again. The truck swerved slightly, but not as much as before. "That's certainly somethin' I haven't been told."

"I just want t' run through the countryside. Period," Megan said.

"I suppose that's why Hugh McConnell wants t' see ya again," Brian said. "He must want t' make sure you're still gonna run the border for us."

"I'm gonna tell 'im I'm not takin' another fool or even the cleverest man in all Ireland over with me again," Megan said. "Bugger their plans."

"I think that fool you had was a special case," Brian said. "Maybe the old man just wants t' thank ya personally. Or maybe he just wants t' hear you tell him what happened yourself. I'm not sure that old man who came t' you at school really knows of any plans. Maybe he was just talkin' in general for the future, t' make ya feel good. They should be tellin' me first about any plans they have for you."

Megan repeated, "All I want t' do is run through the countryside."

"You should be glad they didn't shoot an' kill that fool," Brian said.

"What?" Megan asked.

"Then Hugh McConnell'd be askin' you what were his glorious last dyin' words," Brian said.

"What if he didn't say anything?" Megan asked. "Most shot people cry or make bloody gurgling noises."

Brian shrugged. "They'd make something up, I'm sure," he said. "They'd make up somethin' inspirin' for the cause. That's what they do."

"So, sounds like it would be better for the cause if he had died," Megan said.

"Well, now he's sittin' in prison," Brian said, "an' he knows names an' faces of a lot o' people they'd love t' round up, too."

Megan felt suddenly scared again.

"He's even more o' a problem to us now than he was with just the drawin' o' his face all over," Brian said.

"But," Megan said, "if he'd been a dead hero, everything would be just fine?"

They lapsed into silence for a while, and Megan thought about all the songs of glorious dead heroes they kept playing and singing in all the Catholic bars. A phrase from one of the traditional favorites ran through her head: *"He died for Ireland, and he died for Ireland's freedom, a harp, the shamrock, green, white, and gold..."*

Then Brian suddenly spoke up. "Some o' the old men do great funeral orations. It usually starts with recallin' the first Irish defeat at Kinsdale in 1601. They talk about it as if it were just yesterday. Then they slowly trace their way through our grand history and dead heroes—Roddy McCorley, Kelly from Killan..."

"I know all the heroes," Megan said. "Ya don't have t' name 'em all for me."

Brian stopped the names, but he went on. "Then they work through the Easter Rebellion in 1916, where we finally turned the tide. And they get to the hero they're about t' bury that day. Then someone plays a fittin' tune on the bagpipes, an' some o' the boys, disguised with balaclavas, fire a rifle salute into the air. It all makes ya feel so good about the cause."

"In all the time I've known you, I've never seen you so excited about all that stuff," Megan said.

"Transportin' that boy, an' him gettin' captured, sort of brought it all home t' me," Brian said. "I just sat there in the pub all yesterday, an' I just kept thinkin' about the cause."

"Right, the cause," Megan sort of agreed.

"These things are greater 'n all of us," Brian said. "Don't ya see? I'm part o' it. You're part o' it. Both our fathers were part o' it. An' we've got t' let it carry us t' wherever it leads."

"Right," Megan said again. "An' I'm your Joan of Arc, I suppose?"

Brian smiled. "Sure ya are," he agreed.

"Got news for ya," Megan said. "Everybody 'cept the French think she was nuts, and the Brits burned her at the stake as a witch in 1431. Like I told ya before, I just like t' run."

Brian kept his eyes on the road. Megan could tell he was trying to think of how to reply. *Thank God, he doesn't know enough about Joan of Arc to tell me all about her being some dead French hero, even though she is. She's probably glad she didn't get a rebel song on the bagpipes when the Brits burned her.* "But," she said, "looks like I've got little choice but t' go with it where it takes us, like you said. An' tonight it takes us t' Belfast…" Megan let her voice trail off. She too had nothing more to say.

"Sure it does," Brian then said.

"An' we're almost there," Megan said. But her mind was saying, *Brian's just as crazy as those creepy old men.*

## Chapter Twelve

Brian pulled into the same empty lot they had used before. What appeared to be the same car that met her then was waiting again.

Megan took a deep breath and tried to clear her head. "See you later," she said. She left the truck and crossed to the car. She got in the back seat. The same two men who had taken her to see Hugh McConnell were in the front seat again.

The man next to the driver turned and handed her a balaclava. "The old lady told us t' give ya a fresh one she'd just washed," he said.

Megan held it near her face. It smelled very fresh and clean.

The driver glanced around. "Them's up above seem t' like you."

"God must be smilin' down on you," the other man said.

*Not God, it's the fairies.* She asked, "That bein' the case, then, I don't suppose you'd just let me promise t' keep my eyes closed an' skip puttin' on this stupid thing?"

Both men laughed.

Megan shrugged and pulled the balaclava down backwards over her head. She leaned down, and the car started to move. Despite what Finian O'Farrell's grandfather had said, Megan was still scared of being called before the person she knew as the head man. She would have felt just the same going before the head nun at her school.

The ride seemed mercifully shorter than before. The car turned a number of corners, and then it stopped. It made a wide turn backing up. Then it stopped again. Megan heard a dull thud from somewhere outside, and the engine stopped, as well.

"This time ya stay put where ya are, dearie," the man in front said. "Keep that thing on, but ya can sit up now."

Megan sat up straight in her seat. Someone opened the back door and got in next to her. She smelled the same cigarettes and beer odor she had smelled on Finian O'Farrell's grandfather, but she also detected a bit of the smell of the awful cellar she had met Hugh McConnell in before. The car door across from her closed.

"You can take that thing off now," the voice from the front seat commanded her.

Megan pulled off the balaclava and looked around. She realized they had backed into a big dark garage of some kind, and Hugh McConnell was seated next to her. He smiled.

The two men in front got out, and they walked far enough away to let McConnell speak to her on his own. Megan pushed her hair away from her eyes, but she left the rest of it in a mess.

McConnell spoke up. "I hope you got the word that we're not mad at you or anything," he said. "I heard how you recounted it. We were all afraid he'd do somethin' foolish if things got tight, an' he did."

"I've run into the Brits on the border before,"

Megan said. "I've always done fine on my own. I was always able t' avoid getting their attention. This time they were hidin' and keepin' real quiet. Usually they fidget and talk, or walk along makin' plenty o' noise."

"A unit with good discipline, then," McConnell said. "Would that we had the same."

Megan refrained on commenting on what she felt they did have.

"And you were smart enough t' know what t' do," McConnell went on. "You got away."

"Far as I know, they never knew I was there."

"You've been doin' quite a job for us," McConnell said. "I don't think I thanked you for that when I saw you before. Complete oversight on my part, it was. I forget the nice things when I've got so much goin' on."

"I do my best," Megan said. "I love t' run. At night I use the stars an' the moon t' guide me. I really like runnin' out through the woods an' the countryside."

"But ya must get tired o' crossin' the border all the time," McConnell said.

"No," Megan disagreed. "Runnin' that way's no trouble at all."

"For us, though," McConnell said, "it might be best t' get ya off the border for a while. That fool boy got a good look at you. He hasn't talked, an' I don't predict he will. But he could give 'em a good description of you."

"You're not sendin' me south too?" Megan protested.

"Oh, no...no," McConnell said. He put a reassuring hand on her knee, and Megan recoiled like she had from the hand of the old man at school.

McConnell took his hand away. "No, no, you're

too good for us t' do that," he said. "We're badly needin' your talents here. We have a new job for you in Belfast here."

"A new job?" Megan asked. She had no desire to run through the city streets.

"One o' our lads whose day job deals in used furniture found this old woman who lives with the Prods," McConnell said. "Her mind's kind o' gone, so she's perfect for our plan."

"Plan?" Megan asked.

"We tell her you're a distant cousin," McConnell explained. "You go visit her every other Saturday or so. We don't make it every week. We vary the schedule just like with the runs on the border. She won't remember whether you're really an old relation or not. You help her tidy up the house, take her shoppin', maybe do her shoppin' yourself, whatever she needs. And you spend the night."

"Spend the night?"

"That's when your real work happens," McConnell said. "You talk t' the neighbors, the girls your age. And ya go to the local pub with them. You keep your eyes an' ears open while you're there, an' you report what's goin' on to us."

"That seems pretty simple," Megan said. "But what I like t' do is run through the countryside."

"Oh, you will again," McConnell promised her. "We're just needin' you t' help us take advantage of this opportunity right now. The old woman wouldn't let one o' the boys take care o' her so easy, ya know."

"Well, all right…for a while," Megan agreed hesitantly.

"Once ya go to the pub two, three times, people

won't take notice o' you at all. They won't take any notice at all that you're not one o' them. All kinds o' Prods and Brits go there. Policemen off duty drink, soldiers drink, an' they all talk." The old man shrugged. "An the more they drink, the more they might talk about somethin' they shouldn't. It would be quite a help t' us t' have someone there listenin' if they do. And even if they don't talk about anything of interest, just knowin' their mood and which units the Brits are attached to'll help with plannin' our future moves."

"Makes sense," Megan agreed. Though the idea of soldiers in the bar scared her more than a little.

"Good," McConnell said. "Brian'll get word t' ya about what's next."

"Yes, Brian like always," Megan said. She was relieved he hadn't said it would be Finian O'Farrell's grandfather or some other old man.

Hugh McConnell put his hand on Megan's knee again. She recoiled the same as before. The old man ignored her reaction. "Keep up the good work," he said. He quickly patted her knee and got out of the car and walked away. He gestured to the two men who were still standing a bit away. The driver nodded, and they returned to the car. Megan heard a door open and close, but it was too dark to really see where Hugh McConnell had gone.

"All right, dearie," the driver said after the two men got back in.

Megan realized it meant she was to put the balaclava back on again. She gave a sigh and pulled it back down over her head.

"We'll just be a minute or two while the boys check the street before they open the garage door," the driver said. It was as if he were explaining the delay to a customer in a taxi or a fine limousine.

After a short ride, Megan found herself again on the street in front of Brady's Pub. She got out of the car and waved back at the two men as if a couple of old friends had given her a ride. Brian was on the same stool at the bar, and the same singer was working hard at a rousing rebel song.

Megan walked right up to Brian. "No, no pint before we go," she said even before he even had a chance to say hello or asked if she'd have one. "I want t' leave soon as I go in the loo an' fix my hair."

"Whatever you want," Brian said with a shrug.

Neither said more till Brian had pulled out into traffic and was started on the way home.

"Hugh McConnell wants me t' spy for him in a Protestant bar," Megan said. "He doesn't want me runnin' packs over the border for now."

"What?" Brian said. Again he was taken completely by surprise.

"Says they don't expect that boy t' talk. But they want me off the border for a while. I had a bad feelin' about takin' that boy over from the start."

"Women are better at feelin' stuff than men," Brian said. "I don't know what Hugh McConnell feels, but he's full o' surprises, for sure."

"Am I t' be doin' the kind o' spyin the Brits hang people for?" Megan asked.

"I don't know those finer points o' the law," Brian said. "Firin' squad, gettin' hung…"

"Hanged," Megan corrected him.

"Hung, hanged, shot," Brian said. "It's all the same—ya end up dead."

"At least they don't do the Joan of Arc thing an' burn spies at the stake," Megan said. "The other ways are at least pretty quick." She thought a moment. "Of course, Joan of Arc was burned 'cause they thought she was a witch."

"He's not askin' ya to do witchcraft," Brian said. "Burnin' witches is probably still on the books in Northern Ireland."

Megan thought out loud, "The Brits blamed Joan of Arc's victories when she led the French army on her using witchcraft, an' they say a witch warned James I, King o' the Scots, that if he crossed the water to Saint John's Town for Christmas he would die. The Brits have been a little sensitive t' witches, I think."

"There ya go talkin' about all that stuff I never really learned," Brian complained. "Ya know you did a lot more school than me... Did he die, James I, I mean?"

"Stone cold before the Christmas puddin' was done," Megan said with a smile. "Would that I could do witchcraft."

Brian took his eyes off the road long enough to look over at her. "That's the first time I've seen ya smile in a long time," he said.

Megan met his eyes. She was thinking that maybe her fairies could help her cast a spell or something that would make all the old men go away.

Brian looked back to the road. "How about next weekend?" he said. "How about we go off an' spend the whole weekend together? We haven't done that in a long time."

"You don't buy me flowers, or even a box o' candy anymore," Megan complained.

"If I had a proper job, I'd take ya away every weekend," Brian said. "They pay me expense money for drivin' ya to the border an' all, but that's hardly enough t' cover my pub bill."

"Hardly any o' us Catholics have jobs," Megan agreed. "I've got a job, but it takes most o' what I make t' take care o' my mother and the house."

"Maybe I can borrow a little from my cousin who works in the car shop," Brian said. "Would ya do it if I could?"

"I don't know," Megan said. "All that's happened in the last few days, my head's about t' explode. I can't even think about next weekend. I'm gettin' deeper an' deeper into this cause. Now they're makin' me a spy, and there doesn't seem t' be a way t' turn it around. Maybe what's best for me is t' go runnin' off on my own. I want t' be able t' enjoy goin' off with you. I just need some time t' think without all this stuff goin' on."

"Suit yourself, then," Brian said.

They lapsed into silence. Megan knew he was upset. *That should be the least of my problems right now.*

Megan leaned back in the seat. She tried to doze off into an exhausted sleep for the rest of the ride home, but her mind kept racing. She didn't know any witches, so she kept thinking of how the little people and her fairies might help her with the new twist to her future. But the hills where she loved to run seemed more suited to them than some Belfast bar.

## Chapter Thirteen

Megan found Brian waiting for her again after the end of the next school day. She walked over and opened the passenger side door.

Brian gave her a sheepish smile. "I'm sorry if I pushed ya too hard about the weekend," he said.

Megan got in and pulled the door shut. "I'm sorry too," she said. "I've got a lot on my mind with all that's goin' on."

"Have ya thought it through yet?" Brian asked. "I mean about goin' away for a weekend again, like we used to?"

Megan thought it over for a moment. "Still thinkin'," she answered.

"I'm gonna try harder t' get a steady job," Brian said. "I talked t' two o' my cousins today, an' I went back t' where I dropped off that roofin' stuff t' see if they needed another hand."

"That's good," Megan said in a noncommittal way. "Is that why ya came t' pick me up tonight?"

"Only partly," Brian admitted. "I got word for you today."

"Oh, God," Megan protested. "I don't want t' go see Hugh McConnell or some other old man again tonight."

"No, no," Brian said quickly. "Nobody wants t' see ya tonight." Then he added, "Unless ya'd like t' stop by the pub here in Armaugh an' have a pint or two with me?"

"I'll pass on that tonight," Megan said. "I still haven't caught up on my rest. I'm not sleepin' all that well."

"You will need t' be rested," Brian said. "They contacted me today t' say it's this weekend they want ya t' start with the old lady in Belfast."

"This weekend?" Megan complained. "Hugh McConnell said every week or two. He didn't say I had t' start this weekend."

Brian shrugged. "I only know what they tell me," he said. "I'm t' drive ya up Saturday mornin', then pick ya up same time Sunday. They want ya to leave before the old lady goes t' her church. Ya won't be stayin' there very long."

*Any time there's probably too much time.* She said, "Good, at least it won't be too long."

"Then I report back anything you tell me about what went on in the bar," Brian said.

"I can't imagine I'll hear anythin' worth even tellin'," Megan said.

"You haven't been the same since Hugh McConnell asked ya t' take that boy across," Brian said.

"You're right," Megan agreed. "I was perfectly happy with the way things were. Maybe that's what you should tell Hugh McConnell for me."

"I won't be sayin' that," Brian said. Then he became hopeful. "Maybe they'll put ya back on the border again soon. I don't know what they're gonna do t' get our stuff across without you."

"I sure hope you're right about that," Megan said.

"And, look, maybe we can do somethin' about goin' off on our own the weekend after."

Brian smiled.

"But for tonight," Megan said, "I'll just be glad for a ride home."

Brian didn't argue. He started up the truck and took her home. They agreed on a time for Saturday morning, and he drove away.

Megan stood on the sidewalk a moment. Then she sighed and went in the door, ready to deal with her mother.

## Chapter Fourteen

On Saturday, Brian drove Megan up to Belfast in a dusty black British Ford.

"Can't imagine they'd be worried that your old truck'd give us away in a Prod neighborhood," Megan said.

Brian shrugged. "I get ya there the way they say," he said. He stepped on the gas and frowned. "This piece o' shit couldn't outrun a cow."

Megan laughed. "If they try t' chase us out o' town, I'll remember t' get out an' run."

Brian did not laugh at her joke. He was intent on the road ahead. They had entered the outskirts of Belfast, and they were now taking a different route than he had taken for her meetings with Hugh McConnell. Megan refocused her mind on the task ahead. She realized that running across the border hadn't been anything she had to work at. Being a spy seemed something completely different to her.

They turned down a long street flanked by dull two-floor tenement houses on both sides.

"It's down here," Brian said.

"The houses look pretty much like ours in Armaugh," Megan said.

"They might look the same," Brian said, "but, in this part o' town, the houses are full o' Protestants."

Megan took a deep breath and tried to calm the

tension she felt inside.

Brian dropped her off in front of a door. Then he pulled away as fast as the little car could go. Megan was too focused on other things to even say, "Goodbye."

She stood on the curb and looked at the door. She had dressed in comfortable jeans and a baggy sweater. She had her gym bag in her hand. She had brought a fancier sweater and her best jeans for going to the bar. She also had her running shoes, just in case there was a park or someplace where she could go for a run. The number 124 was on the door. The house was near the middle of the block. Megan went up to the door and knocked.

An old woman opened the door. She stared out of a room that was dark behind her. Her gray eyes and white hair looked just a bit wild. She wore an old cotton housedress and a wool sweater. She had on wool socks that came up to her knees. She also had on old leather shoes that looked like they had been through some war or other.

"I'm Sarah," Megan said. She had chosen a good British name. She would have preferred to use the name of a popular Catholic saint, like Bridget, but she knew better than that. "Didn't they tell ya I was comin'?"

The woman looked back at her as if she were trying to sort things out.

"You are my cousin Victoria, aren't you?" Megan asked. "Ya know, it's been so long since I saw ya last…"

"Oh, yes, dearie," the woman said, and her face broke into a smile. "They said just yesterday you were comin' t' spend the night every Saturday. They said I need a little o' your help since my mind's gone off its edge a bit lately."

"Yes, they told me, off its edge a bit," Megan agreed.

"Come in, then," Victoria said. "No use lettin' the neighbors have too good a look at ya."

Megan glanced quickly over her shoulder. She saw no one.

"Oh, they're watchin' out their windows," Victoria said. "They always are." She stepped back from the doorway and let Megan enter.

Heavy curtains over the front windows kept the front room dark, and it had a strong musty smell. There was furniture piled all around, enough for three or four rooms. A narrow pathway led toward where a light came from the rear.

"Go back t' the kitchen," Victoria said. "Can't sit in my parlor just now. Haven't had a girl like you over for a proper tea in years."

"Where'd all this furniture come from?" Megan asked as she passed through to the kitchen. She identified tables of all sizes, chairs, sofas, and shelf units all piled on each other.

"Oh, it's from here and there," Victoria said as she followed Megan. "My poor late husband, do ya remember him?"

Megan pretended to try remembering. "I didn't really know him well."

"Well, he died," Victoria said.

"That I know. An' the furniture?" Megan asked.

"He used t' haul things for a livin'," Victoria said. "People couldn't pay, he'd bring it all here. Then he went t' work one day, an' he died."

"I see," Megan said. She passed through a door into the kitchen. That room was relatively bright and well furnished. The curtains on the back windows were opened wide. Out back was an overgrown yard.

"So they say you're my cousin," Victoria said after she had followed Megan into the room.

"I'm not exactly sure how the relationship goes. I live with my mum in Armaugh. I teach kids for a livin'."

"You teach the children?" Victoria asked. "In a school?"

"Yes."

"Oh, that's nice," Victoria said. She gestured toward a straight chair at the kitchen table. "Rest yourself, an' I'll make us some tea." Victoria then sat in the chair opposite Megan.

"The family thought it might be nice for me t' come up on Saturday every week or so," Megan said. "I could, ya know, give you a hand at whatever ya might need."

Megan looked around. There were tidy stacked plates on a cupboard across the room. *That's a good sign I won't have to do too much work,* she thought. She said, "They thought I might go to the store for ya, clean up a bit. I have a ride comin' t' take me back before church tomorrow mornin'."

"Ah, a long ride back t' church in yer own town, I see," Victoria said. "A long ride, then a good nap durin' the sermon."

"Yes." Megan smiled.

"It must be nice t' have a motorcar," Victoria continued. "I used t' love t' go ridin' through the country with the young boys. O' course, I was a young girl myself then. Did ya have a nice ride up this mornin'?"

"I did," Megan said. "The sun was shinin' so bright…"

"It was rainin' so bad when ya came last week," Victoria said.

Megan started to contradict her, but she caught herself in time. She realized that was precisely why they had chosen this old woman for her to stay with.

"Yes, it was," Megan agreed. Then she glanced out the window. "The yard looks like it needs a bit o' work," she said. "It'd be a nice day t' work outside."

"Oh, don't mind the yard," Victoria said. "My husband'll clean it up just fine when he gets back from that business trip he's on."

Megan caught herself about to say something about how the old woman had just said her husband had died. "I might help straighten out all that clutter in the front room, then," Megan said.

"No, not that," Victoria dismissed the front room with a wave of her hand. "Your mother's cousin Emory put it all there when the landlord got so upset with how far behind he was with his rent."

Again Megan kept herself from saying something.

"I was even ashamed when I heard how far behind he was," Victoria continued. "Drank all his pay. I'm sure that's how it was. The movers'll be here for it, soon as the church council gets it all straightened out."

Megan smiled. "That's good t' hear."

"Weren't you going t' make me tea?" Victoria asked.

"I'd better put the water on t' boil," Megan said. She went to the stove and picked up the teakettle. She filled it at the sink. Then she set it on the stove to boil.

Megan figured that by the time the water boiled Victoria would probably take over the process as if she had started it in the first place. Megan was getting the hang of how the old woman's mind worked.

"Do any o' the neighbors ever give ya a hand with anything?" Megan asked.

"They watch out for me," Victoria answered. She glanced out the window. "They watch me all the time."

Megan glanced out the window again. There was a high brick wall around the yard. She half expected to see faces peering over the top. The wall itself was in need of repair, just as the yard needed gardening care.

"There's a nice girl next door," Victoria said. She got up and went to the cupboard, where she got a china teapot and prepared it with tea to be ready when the water on the stove would boil.

Victoria turned and took a good look at Megan. "About your age, and hair just about the same color, don't ya know…"

"Who?" Megan started to ask. Then she realized the old woman was still talking about the girl from next door.

"She comes an' goes to the store."

"I want t' meet her," Megan said.

"She'll knock. She always does. You'll recognize her when ya see her."

"I'm sure I will." Megan nodded.

"There's also Martin," Victoria said. "He helps me put out the bin when the dustman comes. I'd never remember the right day if he didn't come knock on my door…" Then she leaned across the table and spoke in a confidential tone. "He's not quite right in the head, they say, that Martin, I mean. But who am I t' say?" She moved back toward the cupboard. "You want milk? Do ya stir your tea?"

"Yes, milk and a spoon, please." Megan nodded.

Victoria brought the china teapot to the table. "I only use good British tea," she said. "Nothin' good ever comes up from the south, ya know."

"Yes," Megan agreed. She felt bold and asked, "What do ya think o' all the troubles?"

"Tuppence and skittles," Victoria said.

"Tuppence and skittles?" Megan repeated.

"Yes." The old woman nodded. "That's what all them politicians got for brains. In their heads, tuppence and skittles is all there is."

The old woman sat down again. She frowned and began to stare at Megan. "Just because my mind's gone doesn't mean I shouldn't remember you better."

"Well, I think we're pretty distant cousins," Megan said.

"Sarah, hmm… O' course I know your mother well. She musta had you when I was over in London. That must be what it was."

"Yes, when you were in London," Megan agreed.

"Don't all you young girls want t' go there t' find yourself a prince?" Victoria asked. "It must be the same in Armaugh as it is here in Belfast. I went over there before they sent all those fine young soldiers over here to help us."

Megan felt a chill at the mention of British soldiers. She made herself focus on the conversation at hand. "Did you find your prince in London?"

"It wasn't for lack o' looking," Victoria said. "Sure, I lived in London for a while." She got up and went to the cupboard for two teacups.

"Was London exciting and grand like they all say?" Megan asked.

"I'm sure it's fine," Victoria said, "if you're a princess or the Queen. But the part I lived in wasn't much different from right here."

"You didn't ride in carriages to the parties and the balls?" Megan asked.

Victoria laughed. "Dearie, we didn't have tuppence t' ride in a cab. An' we had t' pour our own tea."

Victoria then poured them each a cup of tea.

They sipped for a moment. Megan thought the old woman had made her a decent cup of tea.

"The trouble with the troubles," Victoria suddenly said, "is that if those Catholics would stop with their bombs an' throwin' pavin' stones an' things in the streets, even those dumb politicians would find it easier t' solve this thing."

Megan didn't reply.

"O' course," Victoria went on, "I've got more pressin' problems here at hand. All that furniture in there…" She gestured toward the front room. "Man named McKendal had it all on a truck that broke down right outside my door."

"Oh?" Megan said.

"Told me it was too heavy for the truck he had, an' he asked me if he could leave the load here while he went and got another one that was bigger. Then he never come back. What I think is he went right round the corner to the pub."

"There's a pub round the corner?" Megan asked.

"The Cromwell." Victoria said it as if Megan should have known it well. Then she gave Megan a wink. "That's the best place round here for a girl t' find herself a good British soldier, I hear."

"Oh?" Megan said again.

"I wouldn't know, myself," Victoria said. "I never go round there. I never leave this house. But they say the soldiers come up there all the time from the barracks down the road."

"Perhaps I'll go round there and see for myself tonight," Megan said. A lot of soldiers being in the pub she had to spy on was not something Megan wanted to hear.

"Of course what he shoulda done…" Victoria said.

"Done?" Megan asked. "Who done what?"

"McKendal, man with the truck full o' furniture," Victoria said, just a bit irritated that Megan hadn't followed. "What he shoulda done was come back with about twenty good strong men from the pub. They coulda just carried it all away."

"Carried the truck?" Megan asked.

"Well, of course they'd had t' carry it. The wheels wouldn't turn with all that furniture in it. That was the problem."

"Oh, I see," Megan said.

There was a knock on the door.

"If they're lookin' for me, I'm not here," Victoria said. "Unless it's someone with word from McKendal."

Megan put down her teacup and stood up. There was another knock, and Victoria got up too. "I'd better get that," she said. Then she went through the room full of furniture to the door. Megan heard the front door open.

"Ya need anything, Victoria?" a young woman's voice asked. "I'm goin' to the store."

"Come in," Victoria said. "I've got a visitor your age. You should meet her, an' have some tea."

Megan heard the front door close, and a young woman followed Victoria back through the room full of furniture and into the kitchen. She was dressed in jeans and a bulky sweater, just like Megan. She also had dark hair, but it was cut shorter. Victoria busied herself getting another teacup for the newcomer.

"Hi, my name's Elizabeth," the newcomer said.

"I'm Sarah," Megan said. She hoped saying the name sounded natural. It certainly felt weird. "I'm a distant cousin o' Victoria here. The family wants me t' come by on Saturdays now an' again t' make sure she's doing good."

"Not a bad idea," Elizabeth said. "We keep an' eye on her, but some contact from the family is good."

Victoria gave her a disapproving look.

Elizabeth rolled her eyes, and Megan smiled.

Elizabeth got a chair from the front room and joined them at the table.

Victoria got a cup and poured tea for Elizabeth. "I hope it hasn't gone cold," she said. "I'd heat the water again, but I'm waitin' for the truck that's comin' t' take all that furniture away." She leaned in and spoke confidentially. "Some o' it would fetch a really good price in the shops o' London they say…"

"Oh, yes, I know," Elizabeth said. She smiled at Megan. "Where do ya come from?" she asked Megan.

"Just down in Armaugh," Megan answered. She figured naming a familiar place was safest, besides it being the truth for a change. "I live there with my mum. We're on that side o' her family. I'll get a ride back on Sunday mornings before church."

"So, you're spending the night?" Elizabeth asked.

"Yes." Megan nodded.

"Ya know Belfast well?"

"No," Megan answered truthfully again. "Not well at all, actually."

"Ya should come to the pub around the corner with me an' my friends tonight, then," Elizabeth invited her. "Victoria goes t' bed early. I know that for sure."

"I'd love to," Megan accepted. "I was wonderin' what I would do."

"Problem solved, then." Elizabeth smiled. "O' course, since the recent riots an' such, we have a real fun town here… I mean fun if ya call havin' soldiers, an' barriers, an' everybody goin' round 'fraid o' bombs goin' off any kind o' fun. But we still go t' the pub round the corner."

"Things are tense in Armaugh, too," Megan said with a hand gesture that indicated, "What can we do?"

"It's all the stupid Catholics' doin', for sure," Elizabeth said. "If they'd just be happy t' keep their place…"

"We'll have a drink tonight t' our side, then," Megan said quickly. She knew, for sure, she had to change the direction of that conversation. "We can leave all the politics to the men."

"Men, for sure." Elizabeth smiled. "What we all really go for is hopin' t' meet a good man. There are a few o' them round there, an' sometimes one o' us actually gets lucky."

"We will have t' see, now," Megan said. The thought of meeting some strange man of any political persuasion actually scared her even more.

Elizabeth continued, "I guess we're all hopin' t'

catch a good soldier an' go off to an excitin' life in London."

"Yes, magical London," Megan agreed.

"Or anyplace that's better 'n here." Elizabeth laughed. "But we can dream about those things all day. I do have t' get off to the store for me mum. I'll come back round about nine, an' we can walk round together."

"Sounds great," Megan said.

"How 'bout the store?" she asked Victoria.

"Same as always," Victoria said to her. "Money's in the jar on the sideboard. I always wanted t' go t' London. Just once in my life I wish I'd had the chance t' go."

Elizabeth took some money from the jar Victoria had indicated. "See ya later, then," she said. "I'll bring the groceries when I come back t' go to the pub."

"Yes, can't keep Sarah here from her chores, now," Victoria said. She gestured toward the rear window. "So much yard work t' be done out there, an' here she is wastin' a perfectly good weather day. The children'll want t' play out there after church tomorrow. How can I tell 'em no?"

Elizabeth looked at Megan and rolled her eyes. "See ya 'bout nine," she said, and she was gone.

Megan spent some time helping Victoria clean up the kitchen and sort things out, but her mind wasn't in it. She was both worried and excited about what she might find at the pub. The idea of British soldiers being there really scared her, but she was pleased with herself at how she had done so far as a spy.

Megan and Victoria had a supper of leftover beef and potatoes at seven. The old woman continued to talk in circles the whole time. Then Megan excused herself and changed into her best jeans and the good sweater she had brought for the evening. Elizabeth knocked on Victoria's door about nine, as promised.

Elizabeth had changed, as well. Her hair was done up differently, and she wore a tasteful necklace.

"You look nice for a night out," Megan said.

"So do you," Elizabeth returned the compliment. "Now, if we could just find a couple o' men who feel the same…"

They laughed. Megan said a quick, "I'll be back later," to Victoria, and they were off to the pub.

As they walked, Megan was thinking how Elizabeth had no idea it would be the very first time Megan had set foot in a Protestant pub.

Chapter Fifteen

The Cromwell was dimly lit but looked no different, really, than the many Catholic establishments Megan had been to. It smelled of cigarette smoke like all the bars she had ever been in, and was divided into two rooms. In the front was a bar and small tables, and the rear had larger tables and a small stage with a rock band. The younger crowd seemed to be gathered mostly in the front room near the bar. The first thing that really struck Megan was the music. The band in the back was playing a cover of a British pop tune. As the night wore on, she heard them work their way through British and American pop tunes of the day, from the Beatles and Stones songs to the Eagles and Linda Ronstadt. Megan realized eventually that she was hearing not even one Protestant or British political song.

Megan felt the eyes of a number of the patrons as Elizabeth led the way across the front room. They stopped at a table of half a dozen young women. "This is my new friend Sarah, from Armaugh," she introduced Megan. Then she said to Megan, "Let me introduce you to my mates…"

Megan tried her best to remember the names as Elizabeth went around the table for her, but it was difficult, with her being hypersensitive to everything else that was going on and the fact that the process went so fast. They all seemed to accept her right away, so the names didn't seem to matter.

"What'll ya have?" Elizabeth asked.

"What are you all having?" Megan asked.

One of the women laughed. "Oh, dearie," she said. "What we'd all like t' be havin' is one o' those soldiers over at the bar."

Megan looked around at the bar where a number of young men were congregated. It looked like they were mostly drinking beer. She also noticed that a large Union Jack hung amid the shelves of bottles behind the bar.

"But," the young woman continued, "since they don't seem very interested in us, we're all havin' a good pint o' beer."

"That's what I always have anyway." Megan laughed too. She was thinking it wouldn't be so bad after all. She could have a pint or maybe two with these friendly women, and then get the hell out of there.

"I'll get us each a pint," Elizabeth said. Megan reached for her pocketbook, and Elizabeth stopped her. "On me. Next round for us is on you."

"Sure," Megan agreed.

Elizabeth left her and went to the end of the bar. One of the women indicated an empty chair, and Megan sat down.

She declined the offer of a cigarette from one of the women. "A real country girl here," was the reaction.

"I run," Megan said.

"You run?"

"Yes, I won some medals in school. I was on the track team."

Another of the women laughed. "Runnin'," she said with a gesture to the men at the bar, "is the last thing any o' us want t' do from here."

The rest of them at the table laughed, and Megan joined in.

"Don't worry," another assured her. "Ya won't be comin' in your first night here an' go away with a soldier. Ya can sit tight tonight an' not have t' run."

They all laughed again.

Elizabeth brought back their beers. Megan raised hers. "To Belfast," she toasted. "To the newcomer, then," one of the others said, and they all toasted her.

"Although, they seem t' be able t' spot a newcomer," one of the women said. "I've felt them lookin' over here quite a bit since the two o' you came in."

"Do they ever come over an' talk t' us?" Megan asked.

"Sometimes one or two'll give it a try," someone answered, "but they're mostly shy, like our own good Irish boys."

"It's a damn shame, really," Elizabeth said.

Megan looked over at the bar. She was surprised at how they all looked so much like young schoolboys out for a night on the town. They looked so much less frightening without their green uniforms and deadly equipment. One of the soldiers looked about to make a try at catching Megan's eye. She looked quickly away.

A woman said quickly to Megan, "Right, now. Don't stare at 'em, dearie. It's not good form."

The group laughed again, and Megan gave them a smile. She was feeling her reactions had slowed down just a bit with the strength of the beer. *Not good form either to lose my focus here and give myself away.*

The group continued to talk about the soldiers.

"Don't they all look so brave when they're standin' around on the streets with their guns?"

"Ann went off with one o' them last year or so," Elizabeth said to Megan. "He left her preggers, an' they rotated him out t' some NATO operation with the Yanks. She doesn't come round here no more."

This time no one at the table laughed. One of the women raised her glass. "To Ann," she toasted. "To Ann an' her troubles…"

They all drank to the departed member of the group. Megan did as well. She was nearly half through her glass of beer.

"Has anyone ever married a soldier and gone t' London?" Megan asked.

"This is a Highlander unit here now," someone answered. She looked disappointed. "It won't be London with one o' them. It'd be the Highlands o' Scotland. Who'd want t' go there when we've got Ireland?"

"Oh, of course not," Megan agreed.

Elizabeth put down her glass in front of Megan. It was empty. Megan got the hint. It was her turn to buy. Megan's own glass was still almost half full. She set it down and stood up and smiled at Elizabeth. ""I'll get us another round."

"Guess I put that down pretty fast," Elizabeth said. "Thanks."

Megan walked across the room to the bar. She felt a little buzz, but she wasn't really high. "Two pints," she ordered from the bartender, and she waited next to the group of soldiers. It felt very strange being so close to them. She was used to the aura she could feel from the fairies when she ran past their ancient mounds. She had no idea what this feeling might be.

The soldier next to her turned and faced her. He was taller by a head, and he looked very big and strong. "You're new here." He smiled. "I haven't seen you here before."

"Yeah," Megan managed to answer. "I come up from Armaugh t' see an' old relation."

"My name's Andrew," the guy said. "Queen's Own Sixty-First Highland Division."

"I'm Sarah." Megan caught herself just before saying her own name.

"You be back here next Saturday?" Andrew asked.

"Depends on if the family decides the ol' lady I'm visitin' needs me back that soon," Megan answered. She felt more comfortable talking about a topic that was now becoming familiar to her.

"Maybe next Saturday you'd like t' go someplace they have real dancin'?" Andrew asked. "I could meet you here…"

The look he gave Megan made her feel suddenly very special. She fought to recover her voice and said, "Maybe. Maybe if ya bring me flowers, I would."

The idea of flowers had surprised Andrew. He thought about it for a moment and smiled. "Sure."

"Don't be disappointed, now, if I don't come up t' Belfast again next Saturday," Megan warned him. "I won't know till the last minute if the ol' lady needs me here."

"What will I do with the flowers, then?" Andrew asked.

"I'll be back the week after, then," Megan said. "Maybe they'll keep." She had no hope they would. She added, "Maybe ya can give 'em t' one o' me friends over there instead."

Andrew looked over at the table of Protestant women. He frowned and shrugged. "I don't want to go dancing with any of them…just you."

Megan felt a chill. "Well, thanks," she managed to say. "We'll just have t' see…"

"Well, I'll be waitin' here to see you, no matter what," Andrew said. "I'm not like my mates here, who're too shy to ask an Irish girl t' go dancin'."

"Keep 'em in a vase or somethin'." Megan returned the conversation to the flowers.

"I'll try that. I will." Andrew nodded.

Megan was saved when the bartender returned with the pints she had ordered. "Oh," she said. "Here's my beer." She put some money on the bar and picked up the glasses, one in each hand. "Gotta get back t' my mates now," she added.

"See ya next week, maybe?" Andrew said.

"Yes, see ya," Megan agreed. Then she carried the full glasses as best she could back across the room. She didn't want to admit to the slight weakness she felt in her arms and knees.

Megan set the glasses carefully down, then took her seat. It felt good to be seated, as if she were on solid ground again.

"That soldier talked t' you?" Elizabeth said.

Megan did not answer right away. She took a drink from her new glass of beer.

"Yeah, what'd he say?" one of the others prompted her.

The beer helped calm Megan's nerves just a little. *Keep focused,* She told herself. *You're not really among your mates here.*

"We're waitin'," another one said. "What'd he say?"

"He asked if next Saturday I'd like t' go t' a place where they have real dancin'."

"Oh, my God, I'm really jealous," Elizabeth said. "Your first night here, an' a real British soldier asks ya out."

"An' you said...?" one of the women prompted.

"Yeah, what'd ya tell 'im?" another asked.

"I told 'im I'll only come up next week if the family thinks the ol' lady needs me t' come."

"Oh, I'd tell 'em definitely she does," one of the women said with certainty.

"I'll tell 'em if ya don't," Elizabeth offered. "Just tell me who t' call."

"We'll see," Megan said. She took another long drink of the beer.

One of the women across the table stood up. "Who wants another?" she asked. "I'm goin' up to the bar before that poor overworked waitress gets by here again. Maybe he'll turn round and ask me, too."

"Ya can get me one," another said.

Conversation lulled as they watched their brave member cross over to the bar. They all kept watching, but neither Andrew nor any of the other men turned and spoke to her. She returned to the group with two full pints of beer and a look of total disappointment on her face.

"We'll have t' come t' Armaugh an' learn what ya do to have such magic," one of the group said to Megan.

"Maybe it's a bit o' magic." Megan laughed. "When I go runnin' through the countryside, I sometimes feel the presence o' the fairies that people swear are there. That feeling helps keep me runnin' along. Maybe the fairies are helpin' me here, too."

"Maybe ya do have some magic powers." Elizabeth laughed. "Maybe you're really a witch. But don't go tellin' that t' that soldier o' yours, whatever ya do."

"No," Megan agreed. "No, I won't do that."

"Poor Ann thought she was workin' some kind o' magic on that soldier o' hers," one of them said. "She hasn't heard from 'im since he left."

"No," another one added. "The world of fairies an' unicorns, an' that kin'o' shit didn't help her a bit."

"No," Megan said again. "I might be a lot o' things, but I know I'm certainly no magician or witch."

The group laughed. Conversation moved on to others they knew who had come and gone, and this man and that, none of them anyone Megan knew. She quietly drank down more than half the new glass of beer. Time passed, and suddenly all the soldiers left together in a group.

Andrew turned and gave Megan a wave as he moved away. She returned his wave and gave him a smile.

"Well," Elizabeth announced, "I guess all the fun's gone for tonight now. I have t' get up early tomorrow even though it's a Sunday. Come on, Sarah, walk me home."

There was just a second or two of delay before Megan realized that Sarah was her name. "Sure, Elizabeth," she quickly said.

"Ah, isn't your mind somewhere else," one of the women accused her. "I bet we all know where."

Everyone laughed, and Megan smiled. *Sarah, Sarah, I'm Sarah,* she was thinking, *damn beer...*

Outside the air was cooler, and Megan's head quickly felt clearer.

"Ya sure had an interestin' welcome t' Belfast. Are ya all right?" Elizabeth asked her.

"I do feel a bit lightheaded," Megan admitted, telling the truth. "An' it doesn't feel real. It really doesn't. The way he looked at me kind o' made me feel I was meltin' inside an' gave me chills all at the same time, ya know."

"Score one for the new girl!" Elizabeth said, and they both had a laugh.

As they walked along, Megan was thinking how her mother would say that good Catholic girls shouldn't go in those kinds of bars, not even the bars with good Republic of Ireland soldiers in Dublin.

## Chapter Sixteen

Megan was waiting by the curb when Brian arrived as promised the next morning. She had slept, but not all that well. Time dragged after she got up and shared a breakfast of oatmeal and tea while Victoria prattled away. She told the old woman nothing of the happenings at the pub. Megan was very glad to see the beat-up little black car they had given Brian for the transport job. She had spotted it coming more than a block away.

"Good t' see ya safe an' sound," Brian even said as she got into the seat beside him.

"Yes, I made it all right, thank God," Megan agreed.

Brian pulled away from the curb and headed them on their way.

Megan was silent for a moment. Then she spoke up. "Ya still haven't brought me flowers."

"Oh…flowers," Brian said. "Sorry, just not somethin' that's on my mind."

"Right," Megan said.

There was silence again, this time broken by Brian. "How did it go?"

"That old lady I'm stayin' with is totally crazy," Megan said. "Gone round the bend, for sure. Her brain is nothin' but tuppence an' skittles, but we get on quite well."

"That's good ya get on together," Brian said. "What about the pub?"

"It's all really hard work," Megan said. "Hardest part is keepin' your story straight, even with the old lady. My name is Sarah, by the way. Don't be knockin' on her door an' askin' for some Megan in the future."

"Sarah it is," Brian said.

"Yeah, I had t' remember that an' answer t' it with the girls in the pub. When someone says 'Sarah,' it's expected I answer. It's harder than ya might think, actually."

"Sarah," Brian repeated. "I'll remember that. Did ya learn anything for me t' report t' Hugh McConnell?"

"There were some Brits come in there," Megan said. "Someone said they were from some Highland division or regiment or somethin'." She knew she shouldn't tell him a British soldier had taken an interest in her, nor was she ready to, even if she would. *Besides, maybe he's like my fairies. Maybe none of this is real at all.* "You probably know where all the soldiers are from already. They drank round the bar. I sat at a table 'cross the room with a bunch o' girls my age. We had beer."

"Nothin' about what division, what regiment?" Brian asked. "Nothin' like that?"

"They don't care 'bout that sort o' stuff," Megan answered. *And neither really do I.* Still, she remembered very well it was the Queen's Own Sixty-First Highland Division and the very proud way her soldier had said it, as well. "The girls at the table I was at talked about clothes, makeup, an' hair, just like Catholic women do. All they want t' do is find themselves a good man, an' for most o' them a good soldier would be just fine. Most o' them want t' marry a soldier an' move t' London. That's all they care about. But they don't go over an talk t' the soldiers, and the soldiers don't come over an' talk t' them. That old man McConnell's daft if he thinks I'm gonna learn anything important there."

She added, "They had a band." She felt she should elaborate a little more, at least. "They weren't all that good. They just played American an' Brit rock songs."

"No rebel songs, then?" Brian asked, and he laughed at his own joke.

Megan didn't laugh with him, but she did say, "No, not there, for sure."

"McConnell'll have t' be satisfied with that," Brian said. "But you keep goin' back there, an' I bet somebody'll say somethin'. Some information'll come out for you."

"I hope so," Megan said, "after all that work. God, I am so tired. All those lies take more energy than ya know."

"Maybe we could stay over one night together next weekend, if ya don't go back," Brian suggested. "I'll ask about next weekend when I send my report in."

"Might cost ya some flowers, if I do," Megan said. "An' I mean new ones, too. Don't be stealin' me a bunch off some poor sod's restin' place in the graveyard."

"We'll see…" was all Brian would say.

Chapter Seventeen

The week went quickly, and during it came word that Hugh McConnell wanted Megan to go back again with no weekend break in between. She expressed her displeasure to Brian, to no avail, as always. They were headed back to Belfast in the little old car the next Saturday morning, just as they had been the week before.

*No flowers, and a weekend fling with Brian. But then, maybe Andrew won't be wasting a perfectly good bunch of flowers by my not returning.* She had said nothing of Andrew to anyone in Armaugh, not even her fairies. Actually, Megan still wasn't sure the big soldier and the look he had given her had even been part of the real world. She did ask her friend Kate at school if she had ever met a completely strange guy and it felt absolutely magical. Kate's answer had been a simple, "No, not me, for sure." *No help there.*

Brian deposited her and her bag on the curb in front of Victoria's house, and he drove quickly away as before, leaving her completely on her own.

Megan hefted her bag. This time she had brought a little more makeup, as well as her good clothes and good earrings. She didn't really know why the extra makeup, just that a good spy would do what all the women at the bar would expect her to do. *All right, I'm Sarah, damn it.* Then she focused her mind on the task ahead. She crossed the sidewalk and knocked on the door.

Megan imagined Victoria getting up from the kitchen table and making her way through the room full of extra furniture that she was sure was all still there. Then the old woman opened the door.

"Hi, I'm back." Megan smiled.

The old woman frowned.

"I'm Sarah. Don't you remember me from last weekend?"

"You look just like that girl comes here every Saturday," Victoria said. "Yes, she's the one's been comin' for years."

"Right. I was here last weekend," Megan said. "I'm the one."

"Yes, of course, come in." The old woman's demeanor changed. "The family thinks I'm a little off in the noggin, ya know. That's why they send you. You're the only one knows that's not true. Maybe next Saturday ya can sneak off t' Paris or London instead o' comin' here. Have yerself a little fling. I won't tell 'em a thing."

"Perhaps I will." Megan smiled. "But for today I'm here to do whatever ya might need me t' do."

Megan followed the old woman through the room of furniture and into the kitchen, where she sat in the same chair she had occupied before. Victoria went right to work making them tea, and things went pretty much the way they had before.

Elizabeth stopped by in the afternoon.

"Ah, you should take Sarah here to the pub with ya tonight," Victoria said to Elizabeth. "It's no good her sittin' round here watchin' the telly with me every time she comes."

"She did come to the pub with me last weekend," Elizabeth said. "She fooled us all an' actually talked t' one o' the soldiers."

"Oh, yes, of course," Victoria corrected herself. "It must be that other girl that comes I'm thinking about."

Elizabeth looked at Megan and rolled her eyes.

"Soldier, huh?" Victoria continued. "That's what ya need for a good fling." She glanced around. "Think I saw in the paper they're havin' discount fares to Amsterdam next weekend. I'll show ya, if I see it again."

"I'll look into it," Megan promised her.

"I'm gonna get the list an' be off to the store," Elizabeth said. "I'll drop back 'bout nine like I did last week."

"I'll be ready," Megan said.

True to her word, Elizabeth returned just as the clock struck nine.

"That old woman is so crazy," Elizabeth said as she and Megan walked the short distance to the pub.

"I'm gettin' the hang o' it," Megan said.

"We're probably the only thing keepin' her out o' the looney bin," Elizabeth said. "One o' these days I 'spect she'll be dancin' naked on the street, an' they'll finally take her away."

"Speakin' o' dancin'," Megan said. "I told 'im I'd go if he brought me flowers."

"Ya didn't tell us that last week. Think he will?"

Megan laughed. "I've never had a boyfriend that did."

"You're bein' too hard on 'im," Elizabeth said. "I'd go dancin' with any o' those soldiers whether he brought me flowers or not."

They had reached the big wooden door of the Cromwell.

"At least we can have a drink an' dream," Megan said. One part of her brain was hoping Andrew would be there with a big bunch of flowers, waiting to sweep her off her feet. The other part was hoping he wouldn't be there at all.

"Let's see," Elizabeth said with a devilish smile. Then she pushed open the door.

They walked across the bar, orienting themselves to the dim light and loud music from the band. They saw a table with their friends from the week before, across the room. Suddenly one of the men looked around. It was Andrew. He turned completely around, and the two women stopped by him. From behind he produced a small bouquet of flowers, white and red carnations and a few yellow daffodils. He handed them to Megan.

"Will ya come out dancin' with me, then, Sarah?" he asked.

Megan took the flowers. Her knees felt suddenly weak. She was speechless, as well.

"Guess I'll go on an' sit down with me mates over there," Elizabeth said, but neither Andrew nor Megan seemed to hear her. She was left standing and waiting for a reply.

Megan hadn't actually thought out what she might do if he did give her flowers. She managed to say, "Well, I come with my friend here tonight." She looked over at Elizabeth and smiled. "This is Elizabeth. She lives round the corner. An' this is Andrew. He's in the Highlanders."

"The Queen's Own Sixty-First," Andrew said with a gracious nod.

"Pleased t' meet ya," Elizabeth said. Then she added, "Well, like I said, I better go say hi t' our friends over at that table there." She nodded toward the table. Then she moved away, leaving Megan and Andrew alone.

With no beer yet, Megan's mind was totally alert and racing at full speed to recover from the surprise. "It's a little late now to start out for someplace new," she said. "I appreciate the flowers." She held them to her face and breathed in their fragrance, which overrode the smell of cigarette smoke and stale air. "I really do. They're lovely. But I really should have a drink with my friends before we'd go somewhere. I can't just leave 'em without doin' that. An' then it would be even later still before we head out."

"But I brought ya flowers, like ya asked," Andrew said.

"I know. How 'bout next weekend?" Megan asked. "I meet you here earlier, an' I come on my own. Then we go dancin' like I said I would."

"I'm gonna hold ya to that," Andrew said. "But what about tonight? Ya gotta at least have a drink with me."

"I know," Megan said as she got a new idea. "Let's get out o' here for a moment an' take a walk together. I want t' get t' know ya better before I have a drink or go off dancin' with ya."

"Sure," Andrew agreed. "You lead the way."

Megan nodded and headed toward the door. She was thinking what she had just said was certainly true. She sure did want to know him better before she did anything else with this British soldier.

It was cooler and so much less smoky outside the pub. Megan folded her arms and held the flowers as if she would never let them go. Outside she felt a lot safer, too. In her mind, there were few men she didn't think she couldn't outrun.

They walked slowly away from the direction Megan had come from Victoria's house. She again realized how all the houses pretty much looked the same.

"You know I'm a soldier." Andrew spoke up. "But who are you? You told me you come up on weekends from Armaugh, but what do you do down there?"

"I'm a teacher." Megan had enough lies to keep straight. She figured some truth from her real life would be safe.

Andrew was surprised. "You've been through the university?"

Megan gave a shrug. "It's really no big deal." *Actually, for a poor Catholic girl in Northern Ireland to go to college she had to so impress the nuns with her learning that they sent her on scholarship to a good Catholic school in Dublin.* That she knew she couldn't tell him, or that she was teaching with the nuns in a Catholic school.

"I don't think many o' the girls who come to the Cromwell have gone to university," Andrew said. "See, I could tell you were a little different 'n them."

"Really?" Megan asked. She thought she had been fitting in.

"Most girls woulda gone dancin' right away at the first offer. Ya got some real class, or somethin'." Andrew stopped walking and looked at her. "Unless, now, the reason ya turned me down at first is 'cause ya got some boyfriend down in Armaugh, or something?"

"No," Megan lied. "No one regular."

"Is it 'cause you've been t' university, an' I'm just a soldier?"

Megan shook her head. "No, I think we're all the same. You got your skills, an' I've got mine." Then she asked, "When you're out there patrolling, with your guns an' all, do ya ever get scared?"

"Sure," Andrew admitted. "We all do. But when we're out there together we watch out for each other. The real danger is when we don't have our guns and each other. Like right here in Belfast someone might toss a bomb through the window of a pub like the Cromwell, or someone might fire a shot at us from a passin' car."

Megan didn't reply. She had in her mind the image of the bomber she had taken to the border.

"That's the problem with these Catholic rebels," Andrew continued. "No man with a shred o' dignity would shoot another in the back, but that's basically what they do."

Megan shook her head quickly to clear the images she had of the soldiers like Andrew capturing Mick. Andrew took it that she was glancing around. He glanced around too. "This part of Belfast is really safe for us," he said. "That's why we all come to the Cromwell. I've never heard of the Catholics comin' round here."

"Right," Megan agreed. She started walking again, and she decided to change the conversation. "Actually that's got nothin' t' do with dancin'. Sorry I asked the question."

"I forget all about that stuff when I'm dancin'," Andrew said. "But ya wanted t' get to know me better, so I don't mind."

"You goin' t' make a career o' bein' a soldier, then?" Megan asked.

"No," Andrew answered. "I'm savin' my money. When my enlistment's up, I'm goin' back t' my little town in Scotland and open a shop, or maybe I'll run my own pub."

"That sounds nice," Megan said. "I run. I ran track in school, won some medals. I love t' run through the countryside. Most all o' the girls here want t' end up in London, but I hate big cities."

"Me too," Andrew said. "They send us down to patrol near the border sometimes. The countryside here reminds me a lot o' where I'm from in Scotland. It has a school. You could find a job teachin' there."

They both stopped walking and talking, and they looked at each other for a moment.

Andrew spoke up. "Maybe ya won't go dancin' tonight, but at least give me a kiss for the flowers."

Megan held out the flowers. "Ya did give me flowers," she agreed. "That means quite a lot to me."

Then they kissed long and hard.

Megan suddenly broke it off. She pulled back.

"What's wrong?" Andrew asked.

"No, no, I'm not ready tonight for where all this might lead." Megan said. She was kind of breathless. She was upset. "I came up here t' do a job." She spoke quickly. "I came t' help this old lady in the family. I just wanted a drink with some friends at the end o' the day. But it's not like it is with them. I didn't come t' the pub to find me a soldier…"

Andrew laughed. "But when I saw you, I wanted to be caught. I wanted to be caught by you. None of the others seemed to be the one, ya see…"

"Yes, I see," Megan agreed. "An' I don't feel like totally sayin' no. I just need some time t' get my head round all this, t' get myself pointed in a different direction. Tell ya what, next week I'll come an hour earlier. I'll come on my own, an' I'll go dancin' with you then."

Andrew nodded. "You're worth the wait. Next Saturday it'll be."

"Good," Megan said. Then she focused her mind back on the real world. "O' course, the family might not want me up next weekend. If that happens, it'll have t' be the week after."

"Sure, that's fine," Andrew agreed. "'Less a war breaks out or there's riots in Londonderry or some other town around here, I'll be here in Belfast for a while. I'll wait for ya at the pub every Saturday till ya come."

"Good."

They stood in silence again, and Megan felt the urge to just grab him and kiss him all over again. *An' oh,* she didn't add, *by the way, I'm one o' those Catholics ya talk about, and I was sent here by the IRA.* Thinking that helped her make herself turn and start walking back toward the pub. She clutched the flowers tight again.

Andrew walked with her. They walked in silence for a while. Then he spoke up. "The hills are steeper, an' there's probably more of 'em, in Scotland. You'd have t' do some runnin' uphill there."

"That doesn't scare me," Megan said. Thinking of running actually helped her calm down.

"They make us run all the time for our trainin'," Andrew said. "I'll bet I could keep up with you, if you'd let me give it a try."

"Maybe," Megan agreed. She wasn't used to running with anyone, even when she did it for fun. She couldn't remember ever seeing Brian run, except during times of unrest when they all ran after throwing stones and bottles at the police or the soldiers. *Right. An' I just kissed a damn British soldier…an' I think I enjoyed it.*

They had reached the big wooden door of the Cromwell. Andrew pushed it open for her.

Megan gave him a smile. "Next week, then," she said, "or the next, if I don't come then."

"Yes," Andrew answered. Then Megan walked past the other soldiers and men at the bar to the table where Elizabeth and her friends were having their beer. Megan sat down in the one unoccupied chair, and she put the flowers carefully down on the table.

"Your lipstick's a little smudged, dear," one of the women said to her, and there was laughter all around.

Elizabeth stood up. "I'd better get you a beer."

"Yes, thanks," Megan said. "Oh, my God…"

Then she didn't know what else to say. There was so much going on for her, of which she didn't dare say a word.

## Chapter Eighteen

Megan left the flowers with Victoria. She thought of telling the old lady they were from a representative of the Queen, but she didn't want to confuse things more. Megan also volunteered no more information to Brian on the way home than she had the week before. He shrugged and took it the same. By Thursday she had word from him that they wanted her to go that weekend again.

Friday morning, Megan sat in the teacher's room, quietly sipping her tea and thinking out for what seemed like the hundredth time what her response would be if Andrew did take her dancing and he wanted to do more than just kiss at the end.

Kate stood near, scanning the paper. "Brits had t' shoot rubber bullets at some o' our side up in Belfast again last night," she said. "Seems the troubles have reached the point o' throwin' bottles an' pavin' stones again."

"Oh, God," Megan said, and somehow she felt worried for not only those on the Catholic side. She mentally blocked the idea that Andrew might shoot someone.

"At least nobody's set off any bombs for a while," Kate added.

"Yes, thank God," Megan agreed.

Kate folded the paper and tossed it on the work

table they all used. Megan looked around toward the window. Whatever was in the paper about the "troubles," she didn't want to see it. Then she was startled. She saw Finian O'Farrell's grandfather get out of a car that had pulled in to the curb.

*Oh, my God! Is that creepy old man comin' in here t' see me?* Any thoughts of British soldiers were completely gone from her mind.

She briefly entertained the idea of going over and opening the window. It wasn't that high off the ground, and there were bushes below. She could jump out and be gone as soon as the old man went in the school's front door. Even in her good shoes she could get pretty far away before anyone would realize she had actually gone. Not that she should care what he might say to her. But in the far back of her head there had been the awful thought that the IRA would easily shoot someone for far much less than kissing a British soldier.

Across the room, a teacher opened the door. "Megan," she said, "Finian O'Farrell's grandfather's out here. Says he wants t' see you."

Megan knew that if she refused to see him she'd be in trouble with the head nun, as well. She took a deep breath and said, "Tell 'im I'll be right there."

"Maybe he's got his eye on ya," Kate suggested with a devilish smile.

"Maybe he'll take ya t' the pictures sometime," Megan shot back, "if it's not past his bedtime."

"Good luck," Kate wished her.

"Thanks, for sure." Megan smiled. She crossed the room and went out the door.

The old man stood waiting for her. He was seemingly dressed in the same clothes as before. Megan was again repulsed, as she drew nearer, by his cigarette smoke and stale beer smell. He gestured toward the dark corner where they had spoken the first time, and Megan followed him there. She crossed her arms and stood as far away from him as she dared.

"How's that grandson o' mine doin'?" O'Farrell asked in a voice anyone nearby could hear.

"Oh, he's doin' just fine," Megan answered. "One o' me best students as always, for sure."

The old man winked and leaned closer.

"We're really proud o' how you're doin', too," he whispered.

"I haven't learned very much," Megan disagreed. "Nobody there seems t' say much that'd be o' interest for your purposes."

"Ah, no matter, really." The old man brushed it off quickly. "It'll come, don't ya see."

"It doesn't make much sense t' me, really," Megan objected.

"You're clever," O'Farrell assured her. "We know you'll continue t' do really well."

Megan, impatient, felt his effusiveness make her skin crawl.

"I knew we'd spotted a star," O'Farrell continued. "Some o' them thought ya were a little too independent-minded, but you're truly one o' the fighters now, not like the rest o' our women, who take in our boys on the run an' beat the dustbin lids for warnin' when they see the Brits comin'."

Megan didn't want to hear more of that. "Is there a message?" she demanded.

"I just wanted t' tell ya we think things are progressin' just fine, an' for ya t' stay strong to the cause."

"Yes, of course," Megan agreed. "Now, if there's no other message for me this mornin', I got a lot o' things t' do for school."

"Oh, sure," O'Farrell said with more volume again. "Y'd better get on with yer lesson plans. The children just love the stories ya tell." He gave her a big yellow-toothed smile. "It's so good that yer always willin' t' take the time t' keep me informed."

"See you again, then." Megan smiled and backed away.

O'Farrell reached a hand out just short of touching her. He nodded, and he walked slowly away. Megan stood where she was till he had turned the corner at the end of the hall. "Bloody bastards," she said under her breath. *Don't they care I have other things like a real job t' do?*

Kate emerged from the teacher's room behind her. Megan dropped her arms and turned around.

"What'd he want?" Kate asked.

"Well, he didn't ask me out to the pictures," Megan answered. Then she said truthfully, "I don't really know what he wanted. There's nothin' goin' on with his grandson that wasn't the case last time he came. The child is doin' fine."

"Maybe he's a bit balmy," Kate suggested.

"Yes," Megan agreed. "Gone round the bend."

Kate smiled and continued on toward her classroom to start her school day.

*Yes, he's gone round the bend, an' Victoria too. Maybe we all have. I'm goin' back to that pub again tomorrow. An' maybe I'm crazy too.*

## Chapter Nineteen

Brian came by in the little black car to pick Megan up on Saturday morning again. She tossed her gym bag into the back seat and got in. There was a backpack on the floor on her side that made her squeeze her legs a bit to get the door closed. It looked just like the many packs she had carried northward on her runs across the border. "What's that for?" Megan asked.

Brian pulled away from the curb in front of her house, and he began driving intensely. "This weekend, the plan's changed," he said. She realized Brian was tense and upset.

"What?" she asked. "Am I gonna run this pack south instead o' goin' t' Belfast?"

"I wish it was that," Brian answered. "One o' O'Farrell's boys give me this when I picked up the car this mornin'."

Megan looked at the backpack. There was an unusual strap coming out of one of the flaps. Otherwise it looked just like all the rest she had carried.

"It's a bomb."

"What!"

Brian swerved a bit. Then he straightened the car and slowed down just a bit. "Here's how they explained it," Brian said. "Ya go in the pub, an' ya sit it down by your chair, under the table, maybe. Then you pull that extra strap they got comin' out the top. Then ya got ten minutes. Ya go to the loo an' slip out the back door, or ya suddenly remember somethin' ya left somewhere outside. Once out, ya walk, not run, as far away an' as fast as ya can."

Megan found her voice. "Those lyin' bastards… They set me up t' set off a bomb!"

"It's not on you." Brian tried to explain it all away. "The bomb's on McConnell an' his kind. You're just gonna do yer duty like a good soldier…"

"I wasn't sent there to spy," Megan complained. "They didn't care what I heard or saw. They just wanted the people t' get used to me so I could carry in a bloody bomb."

"I'll come back round midnight an' pick ya up at the old lady's house," Brian continued. "Wherever ya go, get back there by then, an' I'll get ya out o' town."

Megan wasn't really listening to him. Her mind was filled with the images of Elizabeth and her friends sitting with their beers, and all the soldiers at the bar. "I'm not gonna do it," she said flatly. "I don't care what happens t' me. I'm not."

"Now, don't say that," Brian almost pleaded. "Look, it'll go fast. It'll all be over before ya know it at all. I even promise I'll buy ya flowers soon as I get me expense money."

"Well, thanks for that." Megan was sarcastic. She realized that arguing with Brian was futile. In his mind, there was just no alternative for her. Her mind raced to come up with a plan of her own.

"Really, the responsibility's on McConnell and them, not you," Brian said again. He said it as if he were trying hard to convince himself of the fact, as well.

Megan ignored him. "Ever hear the story o' Dan, the casket maker?" Megan asked him. "It's not one I tell the children."

Brian did not answer.

Megan continued and told her own version of the old tale. She did it to avoid arguing further and to keep thinking of an alternative plan that would work for her. "Dan, the casket maker, was actually a goodhearted man. He got so tired o' bein' around sadness that he made a deal with the fairies to bring back all the people he had buried over the years so he could throw a big party for them…"

"What's that got t' do with this?" Brian asked.

"I'm gonna make a deal with my fairies t' bring back all the people McConnell an' his lot have killed, an' they're gonna torture him long an' hard…"

"Sure," Brian agreed. "He's the one who's gonna rot in hell for this, not you."

"No," Megan disagreed. "I may end up rottin' in hell for all the lies I've told, but I'm not gonna go there for settin' off any bomb. I said I'm not gonna do it, an' I'm not."

"Ya have no option," was the only response Brian had to give. "Besides, what about all our people starved by the British landlords in the old days and kept from decent jobs by the Protestant business owners right now?"

Megan shook her head. "It's not the same as a bomb."

They lapsed into silence for the rest of the ride. Megan's mind kept working hard. She had brought beer money with her. She was wondering if it would be enough for bus fare back to Armaugh. If only the banks were open on Saturday.

As the two times before, Brian swung into Victoria's street and passed down the block. Unlike the other two times, there was a fairly big truck partly up on the sidewalk near Victoria's door. Brian stopped behind.

Megan got out. She got her gym bag from the rear, but she left the backpack in the car.

Brian grunted his displeasure, and he got out the driver's side. He walked around, reached in, and got the backpack, and he deposited it on the sidewalk next to Megan's feet. "Ten minutes from the time ya pull the strap," he whispered. "Midnight, I'll be back right here." Then he turned and got back in the car.

*Not even a kiss good-bye,* Megan thought as Brian carefully maneuvered around the truck and drove away. *You're a real bastard too.*

Victoria's door opened, and the old woman came out. "Ah, there ya are," she said "I was wonderin' where ya got off to."

"I just got here," Megan said.

"It's all a mess," Victoria said. "Thank God you're here t' sort it out for me."

"What's goin' on?" Megan asked.

"The truck's here for the furniture," Victoria said. She gestured to the truck. "They sent Pat an' his good son Riley t' take it away."

"Oh, good." Megan smiled.

"But they say I gotta pay for them t' do it," Victoria explained. "Reverend McClusky told me for sure it was the church council that would pay. Tuppence an' skittles for brains. That goes for all o' them."

"So where are the men?" Megan asked.

"In the kitchen. I give 'em some tea while we wait for someone t' call back with a straight answer."

"Who'd ya call?" Megan asked.

Everyone." Victoria made a sweeping, all-encompassing gesture with her hands. "The reverend, everyone on the council. They're all tryin' t' find an answer for me."

A man in his fifties or so came out the door. "We've finished our tea," he said. "There's a pub right round the corner. I was thinkin' maybe my son an' me'd have us a bite an' a pint or two while we wait, 'stead o' waitin' here."

"Sure," Megan said. She had an idea.

"This is my relative…" Victoria began, introducing her.

"Sarah," Megan said. "I'm Sarah."

The man nodded his greeting. "Come on, Riley," he called into the house. "The keys are in the truck, in case anyone needs t' move her t' get by. I'm not worried someone would steal an old clunker like her."

"I'll keep an eye on her," Megan promised. Her idea was complete.

A younger man came out the door. The resemblance to the older one clearly showed.

"Before ya go," Megan said to the older man, "which way is the River Lagan? I want t' take a walk along the water while I'm in town."

"The river's that way." The man pointed. "But if ya just want t' see the water, the harbor's just a few blocks down there." He pointed another way.

"Perfect," Megan said.

"All right, mum," the man said to Victoria. "We'll

be round the pub for a bit. Get us word when someone calls."

"Tuppence an' skittles," Victoria said again. "That's all any o' them got for brains."

"Victoria," Megan said, "go back t' the kitchen an' have yourself another cup o' tea. We both need t' calm down. I'm just gonna take a walk for a moment. I need t' clear my head."

"Tuppence an' skittles, for sure," Victoria said with a shake of her head. She turned and went back into the house so upset she left the door open behind her.

Megan bent down quickly and opened her gym bag. She pulled out her running shoes and changed them for the ones she had on. She put the bag just inside the door. Then she took a deep breath and picked up the backpack that was still sitting at the curb. She slung it on, crossed the street, and turned at the corner opposite the way to the Cromwell. She was headed the way she had been directed, toward the harbor.

Megan walked quickly but was careful not to go so fast that she would attract attention. She hoped she wouldn't have to pass through a Catholic area where there might be soldiers patrolling or policemen on the corners. The pack was moderately heavy. The ones she had carried across the border had been various weights, and she suddenly had an awful realization that some of the ones she had carried might have actually been bombs.

*God, they wanted me to take this into a bar full of British soldiers who've been trained to spot unusual things, things like backpacks in bars. They are totally crazy...* Her mind drifted more as she passed along the houses that seemingly all looked the same. *Good*

*Catholic girls don't go down t' the harbor,* she imagined her mother saying. *There's bargemen an' sailors down there. And yes,* Megan saw herself adding, *I'll just pull this strap from my backpack here an' blow 'em all away.* Each block she passed along there was a person or two, people out doing their Saturday chores. But she saw no policemen nor soldiers.

She had only gone a few blocks, though it seemed an eternity, before she saw what looked like a factory ahead. There were some trucks parked on the street here. She knew she had definitely reached a commercial area. The street she was on ended at the big building. Megan decided to turn right, and she walked along it till she came to a side street. Again, she had seen no soldiers nor policemen. Hardly anyone seemed to be around. She looked and saw that it led right down to the water. She reached the end and stood at an old fence rail that was more an afterthought than a useful barrier. The water was a dirty grayish brown. There were some boats out in the harbor, but no one was on the street where she stood.

Megan unslung the backpack and carefully set it down on the ground at her feet. She looked all around once more. There were some seagulls overhead, but no people seemed to be watching her. As far as she could tell, she was alone. There was just enough room for the pack to fit under the bottom rail of the barrier. Megan used her foot to slowly edge it toward the water. It hung out over till its center of gravity reached the point where it tipped and fell into the water. It landed with a splash. Megan looked over and watched it float out for a moment and then slowly sink away. She hoped the water would render the explosive harmless or that nothing would happen if no one ever pulled the strap.

Megan turned and hurried away. She retraced her route back to Victoria's house, resisting the urge to run all the way. She breathed a sigh of relief when she rounded the last corner and saw the old truck was still there.

Megan walked up to Victoria's front door. It was still open. She reached in, grabbed her gym bag, and went over and got in the truck. She breathed another sigh of relief when she found the keys there as well. She had a strong feeling that her fairies were taking good care of her, for sure. She started up the truck and put it in first gear. Megan found the brake and released it. She let out the clutch slowly. The gear caught hard, but she started moving, and she slowly drove away. She made a fairly smooth shift into second gear and gained more speed. The gears were hard to shift, and the truck was a lot bigger that the cars Megan had driven. But she was able to drive it well enough. The gas gauge showed the tank was more than half full.

She had paid enough attention when Brian drove her to figure out the route she needed to go. *I've got till midnight before Brian won't be able to find me. Thank God, or my fairies, that this is an old farm truck or some such. I wouldn't want some big movin' van with a company name in big letters on the side that any fool could spot. This is a lot safer if that guy an' his boy decide to report it stolen.* She kept watch in the mirrors. No police cars appeared behind.

Megan was so focused on her route and driving the truck safely that it hardly sank into her what she was really doing. All she cared about during the drive was getting herself safely away.

She went into Armaugh and found Brian's route toward the border. On a quiet stretch, she let herself take her eyes off the road and her hand off the wheel long enough to glance at her watch. She was doing well, and she wondered if Pat and his good son Riley had yet returned from the pub to find the truck gone. She also wondered if Victoria would even remember that she had been there.

Megan slowed as she reached the place Brian always dropped her off along the hedges on the quiet rural road. She recognized that with no problem at all. She passed the spot and went along to the driveway of the deserted farm where she had always changed in the potato cellar. Megan swung the truck into the drive and took it around to the rear of the house, where the truck wouldn't be easily visible from the entrance or the drive. She let out a long sigh of relief after she had turned off the engine. She pulled up the baggy sweater she was wearing and tried to wipe the steering wheel and gearshift clear of any fingerprints, even though she wasn't sure what difference it would make. "Thank ya much, old truck," she said, and mentally she thanked her fairies as well.

Megan quickly gathered up her flashlight and a few empty water bottles from the potato cellar. She didn't want to leave anything, in case the police might look around when the truck was eventually discovered. She stood for a moment after climbing back out of the cellar. The sky was just at a point where it would start darkening. It was much earlier than when she usually went over. She considered waiting, but she was too anxious to stop moving. Megan slung the strap of her gym bag over her head so that it hung from the shoulder opposite the hip it rested against. Running would be a lot more awkward than with a backpack, but she was resigned to doing the best she could.

Megan took a chance on being spotted and walked quickly back up the road to her usual starting point. Again she made it safely, and soon she was off sprinting across the countryside, though she kept to the tree line and in among the trees as best she could. Passing the first of the old mounds, Megan said her usual thanks and request for a safe journey to her fairies. *God, I hope this isn't really good-bye, at least not to them.* "Please," she said out loud, "at least you guys stay with me."

## Chapter Twenty

Once she was sure she was across the border Megan paused for a while, concealing herself among a stand of trees. She sat and caught her breath as well as let her mind catch up to where she had gotten herself now. She went over everything she had done in her mind. *I had no other option,* she thought. *I have no other now but to go on.* She had decided where she was going next, but she waited till darkness fell before getting up and moving on.

It was a dark, starlit night before Megan reached Colleen's cabin door. She tried to catch her breath as she pounded on the door. It opened a crack after her second knock. The light from inside was enough for Colleen to see who was there, and she pulled the door open wide.

"No one told me ya were comin' tonight." Colleen's face showed her surprise. "I've been wonderin' why you've been away so long…"

"No one knew I was comin' tonight," Megan said. "I come t' ask a favor, a really big favor, actually. I've got myself in quite a bit o' trouble."

"Police after ya?" Colleen asked. She backed away and let Megan in the door.

"No, not them," Megan answered. "Well, yes, maybe them. I had t' steal a truck t' get t' the border. But the ones I'm afraid of are the IRA."

"Oh, my God!" Colleen exclaimed. "How in the world...?"

Megan dropped her bag to the floor and sat in the chair she always sat in. The familiarity of the place and its owner were suddenly quite a relief. "Somethin' I never expected," Megan answered. "They gave me a bomb."

"Oh, my God!" Colleen exclaimed again.

"It was in a backpack like the ones I always carried over. They wanted me to leave it in a pub and kill a whole lot o' people."

Colleen looked quickly at Megan's gym bag on the floor. "What'd ya do with it?" she asked.

"I threw it in Belfast Harbor, an' I ran away," Megan answered. "Or at least I'm in the middle o' runnin' away. I hope it was all right t' come here."

"Sure." Colleen smiled. "You know my loyalty t' the IRA wavers when I want it to." She bent down and gave Megan a hug. "Sure, ya know you're safe with me."

For the first time in a long time Megan started to cry.

Colleen straightened up. "I better fix ya some tea," she said. "I won't even ask if ya want the good whiskey in it this time."

Megan sat quietly while Colleen went to the kitchen. After a bit she stopped crying, pulled up her sweater and dried her eyes, and felt relaxed for the first time since she had been told the backpack was a bomb.

Colleen returned with a steaming cup of spiked tea. "I commend ya for doin' what ya did," she said. "Ya probably saved a lot o' lives."

"They sent me t' this pub so I'd get known,"

Megan said as she breathed in the warm steam and sipped the tea. "The bastards set me up t' deliver the bomb. I started t' make friends with some o' them. How'd they expect me t' blow up people I was gettin' t' know?"

"Were they Prods?"

"Prods an' British soldiers," Megan answered.

"Oh, my God," Colleen said more quietly this time. "They had ya makin' friends with Prods and Brits, and then they give ya a bomb t' blow 'em all away? They are real bastards, for sure."

"Thanks. So I'm not totally balmy?' Megan asked.

"No," Colleen said. "You're a God-damned humanitarian an' a hero, if ya ask me."

"Thanks," Megan said again.

"It's few and far between who defy the IRA," Colleen continued. "What are ya goin' t' do now?"

"That's where the favor you once mentioned comes in," Megan said. "That brother ya mentioned, who gets people on the run t' America? That's the favor I need."

"Sure," Colleen said. "If I ask, he won't betray ya t' the IRA. He's good at what he does. He'll take care o' gettin' ya safely away."

"I've got some savin's in the bank; I was savin' t' buy a nice new car," Megan said. "I'm sure I can access that from here."

"Yeah, It'll cost ya some," Colleen said, "but my brother'll make it work for ya. He always finds a way."

"I haven't had long t' think about it," Megan added, "but I don't think there's anything else I can do."

Colleen had no alternative suggestion. "What about yer mother?" she asked. "What about yer job? What about that boyfriend o' yours?"

Megan was suddenly angry. "That Brian Branigan's just as much a bastard as the rest o' them. He's the one who gave me the bomb. He didn't order it, an' I know he didn't think it up, none of it, actually. But he left me standin' on the street in Belfast with a bomb on the sidewalk at my feet. He told me I had t' do my duty, and he put it down an' just drove away."

"I'd say he's one o' the bastards, for sure," Colleen said, "but your mother must not know anything about any o' this, and surely not the people ya work with at the school?"

"No," Megan said. "I guess I'll be writin' some letters, for sure. Oh, God, that's somethin' I'll have t' think about."

"Well, not for now," Colleen said. She glanced at the clock on the mantel. "I'll call my brother right now. Ya can stay, of course, but they know this is where ya pick up the packs. He'd better take ya to a safer place tomorrow."

"Oh, God..." Megan said again.

****

Megan slept poorly even though she was exhausted. She was sort of half asleep and could tell that dawn had broken when the guest room door suddenly opened. Colleen poked her head in. She was very upset.

"Quick," Colleen ordered. "Make up the bed like no one's been in it, an' hide in the closet."

"What?" Megan asked.

"They're here. I'll try my best t' keep 'em outside."

The door quickly closed. Her friend's urgency gave Megan the sudden rush of energy she needed to jump up and comply.

Colleen crossed the front room to answer the pounding on her front door. "Comin'," she yelled. "Ya don't have t' knock my door down."

Colleen pulled open the door. Finian O'Farrell's old grandfather and three other, much younger, men stood just outside. One of the men had stepped over and was looking in her front room window. There were two cars with their motors running in the drive.

"What's wrong?" Colleen asked.

"Is Megan Bayley here?" the old man demanded.

"Megan?" Colleen did a good job of acting surprised. "She hasn't been here since the last time she picked up a pack for you. I don't remember exactly how long that's been."

"We were just thinkin' she might have come round here," one of the men said.

"No," Colleen lied. "Patty, who brings the packs round, always calls me before she comes. It's never been like she just pops by."

"We need t' talk t' her," the old man said.

"You must," Colleen agreed, "if the likes o' all you came all the way across the border from Armaugh lookin' for her. It's been a year or two, I'm thinkin', since I saw any o' you."

There was an awkward silence as the men thought over their next move.

"I'd invite ya in," Colleen said, "but I haven't cleaned, an' I was out workin' all week. I got a week's dishes in my sink alone. I don't even have food in t' offer. I was t' be off shoppin' later today…"

The men were obviously not interested in her hospitality. "It's very important that we talk t' her,"

O'Farrell repeated, "very important indeed."

"Now what in the world would she know that's so important?" Colleen asked. She wanted to play along by asking a normal question.

"Never you mind, dearie," one of the men said. "We just need t' talk t' her, that's all."

"We thought sure she would have come here," O'Farrell said. "She's nowhere else t' be found anywhere she knows in Armaugh, or Belfast either, for that matter."

"I don't know what she does much or where she goes up north," Colleen said. "Surely I don't know a thing that could help ya,"

"She still might come here," O'Farrell said as if he were thinking out loud. "But I suppose she'd make fools out o' us all, if we waited here an' she didn't show."

One of the men suggested, "Could be she's just layin' low for a while."

"Layin' low from what?" Colleen asked.

"Nothing," O'Farrell said with a sharp look at the man who had made the suggestion. "Nothin' that concerns ya, now."

"Oh," Colleen said.

The other men were glancing around, as if scouting for incriminating footprints or something. Colleen stubbornly stood where she had planted herself firmly in the front door.

O'Farrell spoke again. "What we need is a plan," he said. He looked at Colleen. His riveting eyes scared her more that she was already scared by the presence of all of them. "Tell ya what," the old man continued. "If she does come round, ya call us on the number ya always use for us. But don't go tellin' her we want t' see her, or even that we were here. We want t' make it a bit o' a surprise, don't ya know. Just give her a bit o' tea, an' slip off an' call. Couple o' the boys from Monheghan'll be here right away."

"Right," Colleen agreed. "I certainly want t' be the last person t' ruin some surprise ya have for her."

"Good, then." The old man smiled and winked at Colleen. "I know we can trust you." He reached out a hand and put it on Colleen's arm. It was all Colleen could do to keep from pulling away.

"You'll all have t' come back some time when I'm ready an' set up for havin' company," Colleen said.

"Sure, we'd love to," O'Farrell said. "It'll be quite a pleasure, I'm sure." He gestured with his head, and the men followed him back into the cars. Colleen watched them all get in and start away. Then she stepped back inside and shut the door. She stood with her hands on it till the sound of the cars driving away was gone. Then she started breathing normally again. She opened the door and looked all around, just to make sure they were really all gone. Everything looked as it should be, so she shut the door.

Colleen crossed back to her guest room and opened that door. "It's safe," she said. "Ya can come out now."

Megan slowly came to the front room and sat down.

"It was that old man O'Farrell an' three o' his men," Colleen said. She sat too and quickly recounted what had happened and what had been said.

"Thank you," Megan said.

"No question you're in big trouble with them now," Colleen said. "Let's just hope they keep lookin' up north too. God, I'm gonna have t' go t' confession for all the lies I just told."

"Thanks again," Megan said. "I don't think it's a sin when they're told for a good cause. I think you're just as much a hero here as you say I am."

"Thanks." Colleen smiled.

"An' God, my poor mother," Megan added. "I sure hope they didn't leave one o' their smelly old men waitin' for me in her livin' room."

"I wouldn't put it past 'em," Colleen said. "I'm gonna call my brother back an' tell 'im t' come round by the old cowpath to the back. I don't trust this crowd not t' leave someone on watch where my drive meets the road."

"Good thinking," Megan said. "You should be the one doin' missions instead o' me."

Colleen laughed. "No way," she said. "Our poor mothers keep worryin' about us gettin' pregnant as bein' the very worst thing. They have no idea…"

Despite her situation, Megan laughed too.

# Part Two

# America

## Long Island, New York

"You break the rules, you end up in a dumpster."
*~John Gotti, Jr.*

Chapter Twenty-One

Besides the rebel songs, the Irish had many songs of leaving home. Several of them kept running through Megan's head as she sat, unable to doze off to sleep, on the long flight across the Atlantic Ocean to Kennedy Airport in New York. She had spent her time hiding in Dublin, waiting for documents, reading up on America and the history of those many Irish who had emigrated before her. She read how, about two hundred years before, upstart Americans had stood up to the British and won. At one point British soldiers had occupied Boston and New York City, sort of like Belfast and the other cities of Northern Ireland in her time, Megan thought. *An' there were spies an' heroes among the rebels who were the Yanks in those days.* She read about the Irish potato famine of the 1840s and all those who fled to America, so many that part of New York City had become an Irish city of its own. And she had a current guidebook that even noted the very present "Irish bars" of today, many of which had moved out of New York City to Long Island. Colleen's brother had contacts. They had found her a job on Long Island, in a small town far from the big city. It would be full of summer and weekend people, and the work would be hard. But it would give her a place to stay far below the radar and any danger from the trouble she was in. The only trouble might be that she was not a legal immigrant. Megan had a tourist visa, and when it ran out, her plan was to just stay.

Megan flipped the pages of her New York guidebook to the page that had a copy of the inscription on the Statue of Liberty in New York Harbor. It ended, "I lift my lamp beside the golden door." Megan hoped that lamp would shed light on how she would manage the problem of being an illegal. She knew that many had entered the U.S. that way, and some had found a way to stay. Still, she wondered if the old immigrant dream that anything was possible in America was as unreal for her as the dream of the rebels that some day all of Ireland would be free.

The seatbelt sign flashed on, and the pilot came on the intercom telling everyone they would be landing at Kennedy Airport very soon. Outside the windows, Megan's first view of the skyline and the vastness of New York City appeared. She closed her eyes and leaned back in her seat, saying a prayer to her fairies for strength, in hopes they could still hear her.

\*\*\*\*

Megan changed her currency and bought a cab ride to the Jamaica commuter station that was the one nearest the airport. Then she bought a train ticket with the strange looking new money, and she rode the Long Island Rail Road to the old whaling port of Greenport on the North Fork at the far end of the island from the city. She got off at almost the last stop on the line and stood alone and travel weary on the platform with her bags. A young woman about her age in old jeans and a T-shirt walked up to her.

"You must be Megan," the woman said. "I'm Erin. The boss sent me to pick you up."

"Yes, I'm her." Megan smiled. She had decided to use her own name in the new world and for her new life.

The two women shook hands.

"Ya have an Irish name," Megan said.

"Yeah." Erin laughed. "Some ancestors somewhere back were from there, on my father's side. He sometimes hangs out with the guys he works with at an Irish bar. That's probably where my parents got the name."

Megan nodded, though she found that kind of strange.

Erin took one of Megan's bags and led the way to her car. "So, you're here from Ireland," she said as they walked along.

"That I am." Megan admitted that fact as well.

"Boss never tells us much about the people she takes in," Erin said. We know you need a place to stay for a while, and that's about all."

"Right, that's true," Megan agreed again. "There's a lot o' troubles goin' on in Ireland right now."

"Oh, I don't pay any attention to that stuff on TV," Erin said with a dismissive wave of her hand. "History, politics, I just barely passed all that stuff in school. I went downtown once an' saw the Saint Patrick's Day Parade, but that Guinness beer is too strong for me."

"I've seen your movies an' TV shows," Megan said, "but I think America already seems strange t' me."

They reached an old two-door Chevy Camaro, and Erin opened the trunk for Megan's bags. "It's a '67 Z-28, my big brother's old car. He got married. They had a kid. Now he's got a station wagon. He works construction, makes good money, with all the people moving out here," Erin explained. "This was a really cool car to have when it was new."

"Yeah," Megan agreed, though a Camaro Z-28 meant no more to her than any car. Erin gestured for her to get in, and Megan got in the right passenger side. Like with the cab ride from the airport, driving on the right side of the road seemed all wrong to her.

Erin pulled away and drove through a small business district, then through a more rural area, with beach on one side. On the other side were fields and orchards, but Megan saw none of the grazing lands she had loved in the Irish countryside. There was a bright blue sky with just a few puffy clouds, and there were a few seagulls flying overhead. Megan quickly remembered her first and last awful visit to Belfast Harbor and the seagulls she had seen there.

Erin interrupted her thoughts. "The boss'll put you to work right away," she said. "The summer people are all here now. We need you to do a waitress shift tonight, for sure. Two of the girls have called in already. Must be somebody having a party somewhere."

"Really," Megan said. She looked at her watch. She had set it to local time after landing. It was just getting on to noon. "Guess I've got a little o' that jet lag, but I'll be all right."

"Good," Erin said. "It's all hands on deck when the summer people are here."

The ride ended at an old barn-looking building on the Peconic Bay. It must have been renovated into a bar and restaurant some years before, and had dark red plank sides with white windowsills and doors. The parking lot ended in a short area of tall marsh grass, and beyond was the water, that day a beautiful blue color mirroring the sky.

"This is nice," Megan said as they got out of the car.

Erin laughed. "See what you say at the end of tonight's shift," she said. "Come on in an' meet the boss. Then I'll take you to where you're going to stay."

Megan followed her into the building. The whole place had a rustic nautical theme. There were ship's lanterns, coiled ropes, life preserver rings, and oars on the walls all over, and a carved naked woman from an old ship's bow had been hung over the bar. That bar was almost empty, and only a few of the lunch crowd seemed to be at the tables in the restaurant area. Erin led the way through the bar to a door that led to a rear office.

"Here's Megan," she announced to a fortyish-looking woman who sat behind a desk in a room full of cardboard cases of liquor and wine that was obviously for the bar.

"Hi, I'm Mary." The woman smiled. "We're short today. You don't know how glad I am to see you."

"Glad t' be here," Megan said.

"I'll wait outside," Erin said, and she left them alone.

"Okay," Mary said. "Here's the deal. They don't tell me the details about the people they send for me to take care of. And I don't ask because I don't need to know. I'll be fair and take good care of you as long as you give me a good day's work whenever I need you to work for me."

"Sounds fair," Megan agreed. "I'm a hard worker, t' be sure."

"I've got a small apartment over a detached garage by my house. You can live there, and you can eat all you want in the kitchen here. I'll pay you something, but not a lot, since you get the rest for free."

"That's fine," Megan agreed again.

"The pay's off the books, of course."

"The way I understand things, it has t' be," Megan agreed again.

"Now, when you waitress, you'll get tips," Mary continued. "They're all yours."

"Good." Megan smiled. "Will that be what I'm doin' most?"

"Most, yes." The boss nodded. "But when the prep chef or the dishwasher doesn't come in, it'll be a job for you."

"Right," Megan said.

"There aren't enough people living out here year round to have enough that want to do restaurant work for the summer or even the weekend crowds we get all the time. People who do those jobs, and too many of my waitresses, too, are just not as dependable as I need them to be. They party. They get drunk, partying or not. They get high. They don't show up. I need someone around here I can depend on." She looked Megan directly in the eye. "That's you."

"Right," Megan said again. "I'll do it. I've got nowhere else t' go." In the back of her mind, she was thinking of something she had read in the history book about colonial times in America. It was called indentured servitude. Someone would pay your passage across the sea, and then you would work for them day and night with little or no pay for seven long years in return.

"Good," the boss said. "As long as it works for both of us, you're welcome to stay. Can you wait tables?"

"In Ireland, I was a schoolteacher," Megan said. "I have a college degree."

"Good." Mary smiled. "You'll be a fast learner. Erin will show you what to do out in the dining room, and the chef'll show you how to do the prep, wash lettuce, cut vegetables. I'll show you how the dishwasher works when the time comes."

"Yes, I'll learn," Megan promised.

"Okay, good." Mary seemed to end the interview. Then she thought of one thing more. "It's okay when you waitress. It'll probably get you good tips. But lose that Irish accent you have when you start going around town on your own. The less attention you bring to yourself, the better, I think."

"Surely I will," Megan said… "I mean, okay."

"Good. Watch TV. Watch all the talk-type shows, and the news. There's a TV in your apartment and two of them out in the bar. Football, baseball, they have people describing the action all the time… Not that I don't think it's safe for you here. But there are people around who are funny about illegal immigration, you know. It's just not something that should be advertised, that's all."

"Okay," Megan said again. "I understand."

"We're not an Irish bar, by New York standards. Most of them are farther down the Island, toward the city. But we do have Guinness on tap out at our bar." Mary smiled. "There's a little touch of home for you. You can have a beer on me after the end of your dinner shift tonight."

"Right." Megan thought she'd probably be grateful for that. The boss had made her comfortable enough to add, "Made in Dublin from the waters o' the Liffey River, which some o' my countrymen used t' call the world's largest open sewer."

The boss smiled, shrugged, and continued, "Okay, I can see you'll fit in here just fine. Erin'll get you a couple of the shirts all the waitresses wear. Those jeans and running shoes you've got on'll be fine for the rest. She'll take you over to the garage apartment. You freshen up from your trip and get back here in an hour."

"Right," Megan agreed. In a way, she was glad not to really have a chance to think about what was happening to her and what a strange land she was suddenly in. As she passed back through the bar, she heard a familiar tune. *At least I'm used to this American music they're playing here, from the Protestant bar in Belfast.*

## Chapter Twenty-Two

After two weeks, Megan was well settled in at work. It was hard and often intense, but it kept her mind off Ireland and the trouble she was in. She was so tired that she finally slept well. The food was fascinating, diverse, and a lot of seafood compared to her usual plain Irish fare. The apartment was comfortable, though it was really small. She watched TV intently, and she felt she was becoming bilingual in Irish and American English. Megan's only complaint was that she was terribly lonely.

In the mornings, before the prep and lunch shifts began, Megan tied her hair back and ran along the back roads and on the town beach. With all the summer people who came and went, no one took particular notice of her. The sky was often bright blue, and the sand was various shades of light brown. There were brownish-green sea grass and green trees, but nowhere did she see the greens of Ireland. Some mornings there was fog out over the water, but the mists she loved in the Irish countryside were nowhere to be found. The farms traditionally grew vegetables for the big city. There were orchards and expanses of potato fields that had been tended by many Polish immigrants in an immigration similar to the one of the Irish. Grapes and a new wine industry were now taking root in some of the old potato fields. The Irish had traditionally lived on potatoes, but Megan knew little of wine. However, as a waitress, she was learning about it fast.

The boss finally gave Megan her first day off. Megan went out running in the morning, as usual. The sky was bright blue over the bay, and there were seagulls all around. But there were no ancient mounds where the American fairies might live. She definitely missed feeling their presence when she ran. Mattituck and Cutough were nearby towns with Native American names, but any feel of their former culture seemed very long gone. With the day off, Megan hoped that if she ran long and far enough she might just find her fairies somewhere. She gave up when she reached the congested main road, with its summer people and strip malls of stores.

Megan returned to her apartment and sat alone with the TV off for a while. Then she pulled out a legal pad and a pen she had bought. She had written to her mother and her friend Kate while she was waiting in hiding for her documents in Dublin. The way his actions had declared his loyalty, she figured writing to Brian would just not be safe. The last letter she wanted to write was to Andrew, her British soldier.

Megan knew the name of the street in Belfast where Victoria lived. She was in Number 24. From that Megan knew that her pub friend Elizabeth must live at Number 22. Megan would send a note asking Elizabeth to try to deliver the letter to Andrew at the pub and include just a brief letter to Andrew. She was afraid to put a return address, but the postmark would tell them she was in America.

After a false start or two, Megan wrote, "Dear Andrew, I hope you won't think me horrible to have left you the way I did. Something came up from my past, and I am now in America. I want you to know I wish I could have stayed. Thank you again for the lovely flowers. I wish very much we could have gone dancing." She thought a moment. Then she signed it, "Love, Sarah." *There,* Megan thought. *That's enough for me to say. Now, I'm going to walk down to the post office and mail this off before I lose my nerve.*

\*\*\*\*

Megan cried a little, slept a little, and watched TV. When the time came that the dinner shift was usually over, she walked to the restaurant. She'd decided to treat herself to a Guinness even if she hadn't worked that day.

The bar was empty when she got there, and the last customers were leaving the restaurant. Erin had served that last table. She passed Megan on her way to the kitchen.

"Can't stay away from here, huh?" she asked.

"No." Megan smiled. "I guess I want my usual end-o'-the-day beer."

"I'll have one with you," Erin said, "soon as I check in the kitchen."

Erin went in back. John, the old bartender, brought Megan her "usual." He set a Bud Light at the place next to Megan. He had heard Erin and knew it was Erin's usual. "Not on the house, if you're not working," he said. "But I already started closing down. So you owe me tomorrow."

"Sure," Megan agreed. John went to the cash register and continued his business there.

Erin came out with two plates of food. She set one in front of Megan.

Megan sniffed it and frowned.

"Calamari," Erin said. "Chef had extra to get rid of. It's on the menu. You must have served plenty of it. Don't tell me you've never had it."

"I don't eat everything this kitchen makes," Megan said.

"It's beer-battered fried squid. It's Italian, actually," Erin explained. "That's part of Europe, like Ireland. I know that much about the world. It goes great with good American beer."

"Okay." Megan laughed. She tried a piece. "It not so bad." She washed it down with a drink of her Irish beer. Then she added, "Traditionally, in Ireland, we call seafood famine food. It's sort of the last thing anybody wants to eat."

"You people are missing so much," Erin said. "It's a God-damned shame."

They both laughed.

"Try the next one with the sauce," Erin said, and she demonstrated with a big bite of her own.

Megan took another bite, with the sauce this time. "Okay," she said. "I'm American now."

Erin looked around. Only John was anywhere near, and he was totally focused on his receipts for the day. "You know, you can tell me it's none of my business, if you want, and I won't be offended, but I don't think you are even here legal."

"No?" Megan asked surprised by the sudden question.

"I know what the boss is doing. I bet you're an illegal immigrant like the Mexican guy who does prep in the kitchen."

Megan took a long drink from her beer before she

answered. "I promised myself I wouldn't lie so much in my new life," she said. "I trust you. The answer to that question is a yes. I only have a tourist visa."

"Right," Erin said. "I can always tell. Trouble is, none of them ever stay very long."

There was a silence for a moment, and they both took drinks of their beer. Megan was waiting for Erin to ask why.

"I got in some trouble in Ireland, an' I had t' leave," Megan explained.

"Man trouble?" Erin asked. "Like you were ballin' somebody's husband, or something?"

"No." Megan laughed. "I wish it were so simple. No, my trouble had to do with one of the things you don't like. Let's just say it involved politics."

"Oh, yes, that and history," Erin agreed.

Megan nodded. "Yes, I think we Irish pay too much attention to our history."

"What's really important is today," Erin said. "Now that I know your story, I'm gonna worry about you getting caught by Immigration. I mean, it doesn't happen often, but you talking with that Irish accent of yours might just get some tourist or one of the summer people to call the police tip line or something. Some of the people we get in here aren't all that friendly to immigrants like the boss and the rest of us who work here are. What you need to do is become an American so you can stay."

"Yes," Megan agreed. "That's what I should do. I could even work legal, then. But I haven't even started to figure out how."

"Hell, I was born here," Erin said, "right up in the hospital in Greenport. Being an American just happened, for me. The easiest way for you is to just marry an American. It happens all the time."

"I have a feelin' that's easier said than done," Megan said.

Erin thought about it for a moment. "Right," she agreed. "You certainly wouldn't want to marry someone like that skuzzy dishwasher we have in the kitchen. The chef and both bartenders are spoken for, and so's my brother and all my old high school friends…"

"There are a few guys who hang around the bar on a regular basis," Megan noted. "I don't think I see any women with them most of the time."

"Oh, you wouldn't want any of them, either." Erin dismissed the thought with a wave of her hand. "I do my best to hide when any of them try to hit on me."

"Back in the old days in Ireland they had matchmakers who decided who you'd marry."

"I never heard of that. I sure wouldn't want that."

"Neither would I." Megan laughed. "So, that's my problem, then. If scoutin' the bars and workplaces is the way I have t' do it, how does one get a candidate who's worth the while?"

"I haven't done so well in that department myself," Erin admitted. "I've had more than a couple of boyfriends, but none of them ever stayed around. I don't think I ever really felt the magic people talk about with any of them, either."

"I sort of did, just briefly," Megan said. "I met this really great guy, but then I had t' leave."

"Bummer," Erin agreed.

"Before that, I had a boyfriend for a real long time, guy I grew up with," Megan said. "There was some magic, but lately I took a good look at 'im, an' it kind o' went far away."

"Bummer even more."

"You know, I wonder what those places you all call Irish bars over here are really like. What kind o' men go there?"

Erin shrugged. "I'm sure they all have Guinness on tap. Besides that, maybe what we call Irish food and a few flags, photos, and stuff on the walls. The few I've been in aren't really different than here." She thought and then added, "Maybe the music is Irish, I mean, I guess they do have a little different atmosphere…"

Megan smiled. "I haven't hardly heard any real Irish music since I got on the plane." She took a long drink of beer, as if that might help her remember.

"There's no place like that right around here," Erin said. "But there is one down in Riverhead. It's called Clancy's."

Megan nodded. "That's a good Irish name."

"Tell ya what." Erin smiled. "My brother lives down in Riverhead. I sometimes babysit for him an' his wife. I owe him a lot of nights for the car he gave me. If the boss'll let us both off on the same night, I'll drop ya off and bring ya back."

"Okay, you got a deal." Megan lifted her glass in a salute, and Erin did the same.

"That is, if you don't mind walking into a strange bar alone," Erin added.

"Believe me, I've done that before. A lot worse, actually," Megan said.

"What did you do in Ireland, anyway? What kind of job did you have, I mean?"

"I was a schoolteacher. I taught the little kids."

"A teacher!" Erin exclaimed. "A teacher, an' here you are washing dishes, prepping, and waiting tables, and not getting an American's full pay."

"One does what one must," Megan said. "But that sounds like philosophy, which I'm sure isn't your thing either."

"A teacher. You must have been to college."

"I've been there," Megan admitted with an ironic smile. "An' that's not as common for the part of Ireland I'm from as even around here."

"No wonder you know all about history and politics," Erin said. "You must know a lot of stuff…"

"I used to teach my children the old legends of Ireland. An' I taught 'em about the fairies that appear out o' the mists on the hills in the morning."

"Really!" Erin was amazed. "I would have never known."

"The good Saint Patrick was said t' have been put to sleep by fairy music on the eve of Samhain…"

"Really?" Erin said again.

"But enough o' that." Megan laughed. "I need more beer t' tell ya all about the world o' fairies, an' witches, an' legends, and I don't want to have more than one of these strong Irish beers." Megan looked at her glass. "This stuff is a lot stronger than that stuff you all drink, an' I want t' walk straight goin' home."

'You go to an Irish bar looking for a good man," Erin warned, "you order a Bud Light and keep your brain in top shape."

"I'll remember that," Megan said, and they toasted with the last of the beer in their glasses.

## Chapter Twenty-Three

The sign above the door read "Clancy's Irish Pub." Megan paused for a deep breath, with her hand on the door. *What the hell, at least this place'll be full o' Yanks, not Prods an' Brits.*

Megan was dressed in a tank top and shorts, just like the rest of the casually dressed clientele in the bar. The place didn't look much different from the restaurant and bar she worked in, except for a big Republic of Ireland flag on the wall behind the bar and old photos of Irish tourist sights, mostly in Dublin, on the walls. Also, just like in the restaurant where she worked, men and women mixed freely with each other. There appeared to be just as many women as men at the bar. Megan knew she should have known it would be a restaurant and bar full of Americans, but it certainly didn't have the feel of home she had been hoping to find.

There was an "Irish" folk group performing on a little stage that night. Two guys and a woman, all in their forties and playing guitars. One guy wore an old silk top hat. They all sang, and sometimes one of them would play a wooden flute. They were working their way through one of the many sad songs of the immigrants leaving Ireland for America.

Megan spotted a single empty stool at the bar. She took another deep breath and crossed over to claim it for herself. There was a woman on her left who was engaged in a deep conversation with a man next to her. On Megan's right was a man who seemed to be alone. Probably a little older than Megan, he had dirty blonde hair and the build of a construction worker. He smiled at her as she climbed up on the stool. Megan smiled back, and she noted that he had kind-looking eyes.

The bartender arrived on the other side of the bar, and Megan ordered herself a Bud Lite. She noted that people on both sides of her were drinking dark-looking beers that were no doubt Irish Guinness. The guy didn't say anything, and Megan listened to the music while she waited for her beer to come. While she did, the folk group launched into a rousing rebel song. *Now I should really feel at home.*

Megan put a twenty-dollar bill down on the bar. She noticed a Mason jar a little down from her on the bar. It was stuffed with bills of various denominations. She was going to leave a tip on the bar in front of her when she got the change from her twenty. She hadn't seen any jars like that on the bar where she worked.

Megan spoke up. "What's that jar for?" she asked the guy next to her.

"Oh, they're collecting tonight for the Northern Ireland Relief Fund again," he said.

"Oh," Megan said, surprised.

"Wait till they finish this one about the boys marchin' at dawn," the guy explained. "They'll give their little spiel. Then they'll pass that guy's top hat, as well."

"Oh," Megan said again, this time as if she completely understood. Her beer came, and she took a couple of sips. It tasted a lot different than Guinness.

*God, I should've tried one of these before I came here.*

The group completed the song, and everyone cheered.

"Up the Republic!" the singer with the hat yelled.

There were a few more cheers.

The other man took the microphone. "Tommy's gonna take off his hat now…"

"Just his hat?" someone yelled.

There was laughter.

The woman on stage leaned over and spoke into the microphone. "There's nothing more worth seein', trust me," she said.

Some of the crowd laughed again.

"I'm tryin' t' be serious now," the other singer continued. "If ya love the songs we've been singin', an' ya love Ireland, we want ya t' give a little o' your American green to the relief fund for Catholic Belfast."

There were both groans and a few scattered cheers.

"Ya might have noticed there's jars all around, an' Tommy's gonna pass 'is hat around, as well. Please, it goes for the widows an' children, who suffer most from the troubles."

The man next to Megan looked around at her. "The boss here is always collecting for the fund," he said. "He says he has relatives over there, but I think the money goes to guns for the IRA."

"You don't say," Megan said. "God, those singers have such bad fake Irish accents."

Someone from one of the tables passed the hat to the man next to Megan. He left it empty and passed it to her. Megan did the same, setting it in front of the woman on the side of her opposite from the guy she was talking to.

"You know," the guy said. "I detect just a bit of Irish accent with you."

"Really?" Megan acted surprised. She thought she was doing much better than that. "Are you Irish?" she asked.

"No." The guy laughed. "But my grandfather's parents came over. Went through Ellis Island in the harbor here. Yours come over too, then?"

"No, actually they didn't."

"So then you are Irish," the guy said.

"You got it," Megan admitted. She figured that part of her story would be safe to tell. She figured she could get away with saying she was a tourist in the bar.

"Then what are you doing drinking a Bud Lite there?" the guy asked.

"You're right," Megan agreed, "but a girl doesn't want a strong beer going to her head in a strange bar." She took another sip and added, "It does kind of taste like sewer water to me."

The guy laughed. He raised his glass. "Guinness," he said, "brewed at Saint James Gate in Dublin with water from the Liffey River, world's biggest open sewer."

"Where'd you hear that?" Megan asked.

"Oh, somewhere around," he answered.

"Are you sure you've never been to Ireland?" Megan asked.

"No, never," the guy said. "Place I'd like to see is Belfast."

"Really?" *Of all the places in Ireland, he picks Belfast.*

"Yeah, I want to see the Harlan and Wolff Shipyard, place where they built the *Titanic*. The whole story of how they built an unsinkable ship that sank on its maiden voyage has always fascinated me. You ever been to Belfast?"

"Mostly in the residential parts." Megan told the truth. She took another sip of her beer. *An' of course I disposed of a bomb in the harbor, but I didn't stop t' look around.*

The guy smiled. "Hey, let me buy you a real Guinness. Just leave that stuff you're drinking." He looked around at the bartender, who was not far away. "Hey, Patrick," he called. "Get this woman here a Guinness on me. I just discovered she's from Ireland."

The bartender came over. "Oh, really," he said. "What's your name?"

"Megan," was all she gave him.

"Megan, huh," he repeated, and he fixed her with a hard look that gave her a quick chill. Then he looked away and walked to his beer taps.

"Megan, huh," the guy next to her said, recapturing her attention. "Good Irish name. My name is Sam." He held out his hand. "Like Uncle Sam, born on the Fourth of July."

Megan shook his hand.

"Just kidding about the Fourth of July birthday," Sam continued, "but I'm American as they come. I just like the beer and the music here. I don't really know much about the old country."

"That bartender's kind of weird," Megan said. "Maybe a little scary, really. That look he gave me…"

"Oh, don't mind Patrick." Sam dismissed her concern with a wave of his hand. "He's got connections with the old country. He's always a little suspicious of people claiming to be from there who really aren't."

"Hmm, you don't say…"

The bartender returned with a good frothy Guinness. He put it down in front of Megan, and he waited while she took a first sip.

Megan looked up at him and said, "Thanks, that was good." As she did, Patrick lifted a small camera and snapped her picture. "Hey!" Megan protested. "Why'd you do that? I didn't say ya could."

"I like to put up the pictures of all the people who come in here and say they're from Ireland," Patrick explained with a smile. He gestured to a big mirror behind the bar under the Irish flag. Megan hadn't noticed before, but there were a number of photos stuffed in the molding around the edges of the mirror. There appeared to be both men and women of all ages, some of them posed and some not at all, like her.

"No harm in helpin' me with a little advertising." Patrick shrugged. "Sam, I'll make the Guinness on the house for her."

"Thanks," Sam said.

"Makes this place more valid if newcomers know that real Irish people come here," the bartender explained.

Megan sipped more of her beer. She didn't agree.

"Where you from?" Patrick asked.

"Monheghan," Megan lied. She figured it would be safer to say she was from the independent part of Ireland.

"You here for long?"

"Visiting friends," Megan explained. "They had somewhere to go tonight, so I came in here."

"Welcome, then," Patrick said with a sudden giant smile and a magnanimous arms-spread-wide gesture.

Megan wasn't convinced of his sincerity.

Someone down the bar called for another drink. The bartender smiled again and moved away.

"That's our Patrick." Sam spoke up. "He's quite a character."

"I don't like him taking my picture," Megan said. "Gives me the creeps."

"All in good fun." Sam laughed. "He just loves to brag on how many real Irish people come here. Besides, if he'd asked you to pose, you'd probably have said no and covered your face or something. One couple from Dublin practically ran out of here one night when he asked them. He's just gotten more clever in his old age."

"Old age?" Megan asked. "He doesn't look any older than you."

Sam laughed again. "I'll take that as a compliment."

Megan decided to change the subject. "Actually, in addition to visiting friends, I'm working on a thesis for my graduate studies," she said. "I'm comparing our fairy stories with your Native American lore."

"No fairies here on Long Island," Sam said. "The only fairies in New York are the queers, and they're mostly on Fire Island or down in the city."

Megan laughed. "You Americans just don't have the sense of history that we do. Fairies mean old times and magical things to us in Ireland."

Sam shrugged. "The hurricane of '38 and rum-running in the Prohibition days is the only history we ever talk about around here."

*All his interest in history is with disasters and gangster movie stuff. These Americans...* She remained silent, and she sipped her beer.

The folk group started up again. They launched into a traditional song about a dying rebel.

"He died for Ireland, and Ireland's freedom, the harp, the shamrock, green, white, and gold." Megan caught herself softly singing along. For just a moment the song and the beer had made her feel just a little bit at home. Then they launched into a more lively one, a comic song, about the Devil joining the British army.

Megan looked at her watch. It was almost time for her to go outside and meet Erin. *This guy's not asking me to go dancing, and I'm not gonna hint that he should bring me flowers. I do know men do that here in America, too.* She finished the rest of her Irish beer.

"It's almost time for me to go outside and meet my ride," Megan said to Sam. "It's been nice meeting you here tonight. Thanks for offering to buy me the beer."

"Sure." Sam smiled. "Will I see you here again before you go home?"

"You never know." Megan smiled back. "Next week, maybe. I'll look for you when I come."

They nodded to each other. Then she pushed off her stool and headed out the door.

The cooler night air outside felt good. It was not long before Erin pulled up in front of her.

"How'd it go?" Erin asked when they were on their way. "How'd you do with our Ireland in America?"

"Okay, I guess," Megan said. "But I'm not sure I'll go back there. I need to think it over." *Yes, I need to take a nice long run and talk it over with my fairies, even if they're not really over here.*

"That doesn't sound so good," Erin said.

"The bartender was really obnoxious."

"Did he try to hit on you?"

"No, not that."

Erin laughed. "Just remember, like when you're waitressing, since times changed in the sixties, us American girls don't take any shit."

"Yes," Megan agreed. "I'll remember that."

## Chapter Twenty-Four

A few days later, Megan showed up for work at midmorning as usual. She walked in the door and started past the bar toward the kitchen. John, the bartender, stopped her.

"Megan, hold up," he said in a worried tone.

"What?" she asked.

"There's two men sitting in the restaurant over there who want to talk to you."

Megan looked over. There were two men seated at one of the tables. They were in their late thirties and were dressed like any of the tourists or summer people in town. Megan frowned. "Who are they?"

"Nobody I know," John said. He shrugged. "But they look like they mean business, whoever they are."

Megan looked back at the men. The restaurant wasn't open yet. There was no other reason for them to be sitting there. She was sure, too, their reason wouldn't be anything good for her. For a brief second she thought of looking away. Like in her story of the old lady and the fairy, she was hoping when she looked back they, like the magical fairy, would have gone away.

"They said they wanted to talk to the waitress here that has an Irish accent," John added. "That's you. You better go see what they want. I'll keep an eye on them and you."

"Thanks," Megan said. She took a deep breath and walked over to the two men. As she approached, she felt they were looking at her, assessing her, almost in a clinical manner.

"You asked to see me?" Megan managed to say in her very best American accent.

"Yes," one of the men said. Both of them stood up and pulled out IDs. "We're with the FBI. I'm Agent Burton, and this is Agent McGuire."

Megan had a sudden very sick feeling in her stomach. She took a step back, her mind racing, calculating the distance to the door and the chance of outrunning them, but to where? Megan decided to hold her ground.

"Can we ask you a couple questions?" Burton asked. He was obviously the one in charge.

They took Megan's silence as a "yes." She was almost in a panic, imagining herself locked up in New York City with all the streetwalkers and addicts, like she had seen on TV.

The agent gestured for her to sit down at their table, and they all sat down. Megan felt better. Her knees had started to shake.

"Do you have ID?" Burton asked.

"I don't have it with me," Megan managed to say. "It's back where I'm staying. It's just down the road."

"Okay," McGuire said. "We'll stop and have a look before we're done."

"So, when we look at it," Burton asked. "What do we see?"

"I won't lie to you," Megan said. "I'm an unwilling citizen of the British Empire. I'm a Catholic from Northern Ireland. I came here on a tourist visa. I got everything to show that's legal."

"But you're working here. You're not a tourist, are you?"

"I got in some trouble with the IRA," Megan explained. "I had to run away. I can't go back. I need to work to earn my way."

The two men looked at each other. "Get her asylum?" McGuire asked.

Burton shrugged. "Perfect for our purposes."

Megan was too scared to wonder what that might mean.

Burton looked back at her. "Okay, Megan. It's Megan, isn't it?"

"Yeah, that's my real name." Megan nodded.

"We've got all we need to take you into custody and investigate further. We'll probably find enough to turn you over to Immigration, and they will likely send you back to Northern Ireland."

Megan did not respond. She knew her face was probably completely white.

"But," Burton continued, "talk to us, and we might be able to work out some other kind of deal."

"Deal?" Megan frowned.

"First, I better tell you your rights," McGuire said. He went through the standard Miranda rights speech in a well-used monotone. "Do you understand?" he asked when he was done.

"Means I can keep quiet and get a lawyer?" Megan asked.

"Yep," McGuire agreed. "You got it. I can tell you're pretty sharp."

Megan didn't thank him for the compliment. But she asked, "Talk about what?"

"Okay, we'll talk," Burton said. "But you can stop at any time."

"Okay," Megan agreed.

"What kind of trouble did you get in with the IRA?" Burton asked.

Megan shrugged. She figured the whole story would be the best for her to tell. "They sent me to this Protestant pub in Belfast, first as a spy, then to leave a bomb. I drew the line there. I told them I wasn't gonna leave their bomb. I dumped it in Belfast Harbor, an' I ran away."

The two men looked at each other again. "Wow," McGuire said.

"Okay," Burton said. "Here's the deal. We got this tip. We can't tell you who, how, or where it came from, but word was there was this Irish waitress working illegal in this restaurant here. We had no idea you had run afoul of the IRA. That's a real extra for us here. You see, we need somebody who is genuinely Irish to snoop around a certain bar for us."

"Snoop around a bar?" Megan asked.

"Technically, you'd be what we call an informant," McGuire explained.

"Irish bar called Clancy's, down in Riverhead," Burton continued.

"I was there once," Megan said.

"Good." Burton smiled. "We know they're collecting money. We think it's part of a big operation that's supplying guns and bomb materials to the IRA."

McGuire laughed. "It appears you've got real experience on the other end with that, and you say you were even spying for them in a pub…"

"We've gone in, men and women both,

undercover, but they seem to be able to spot a fake Irishman every time," Burton continued. We need someone who's really Irish to make friends, talk a bit, and find out what the real story with the money is."

"They say it's for NORAID, the Northern Ireland Aid Society," McGuire added. "They're set up as a legitimate charity, all legal and everything. They even have a headquarters in the Bronx. They've raised millions of dollars over the years, for the widows and children over there, so they say. And maybe they have. But the British know there's also millions funding the Catholic side in all the trouble over there now."

"Yes," Megan agreed. "I do know about some of the IRA part of that first hand, for sure. They have guns and bombs. But I never knew where the money for them came from. Nobody on my level cares about that sort of thing."

"We just need a few names of who might be involved," Burton said. "Or maybe what someone might say that would be incriminating or lead us to someone or somewhere."

"They passed a hat, an' they had collection jars on the bar the night I went there," Megan said. "Told us it was for the widows an' children in Belfast who were victims o' the troubles."

"Yeah, we saw that for ourselves," McGuire said. "Burton an' I went there one night pretending to be tourists. Hell, I've even got an Irish last name. But nobody seemed interested in giving us even the time of day."

Megan smiled despite her situation. "The creepy bartender there acted like I was special since I was from the old country," Megan said. "I went into a pub full o'

Prods and Brits in Belfast. I can certainly go back to Clancy's and snoop around for you."

"Us FBI aren't always treated as the best people in the world," Burton said. "But I can guarantee you we're not gonna send you back there to leave any bombs. We're the ones who track down the bombers. That's what we do."

"Were you planning to go back there any day soon?" McGuire asked.

"Me and my friend Erin here both have to have the night off," Megan said. "Erin babysits for her brother in Riverhead, but she's my ride down there. We'll probably be off next Wednesday."

"Okay," McGuire said. He gave Megan his business card. "Call us and let us know for sure. In fact, there's an emergency number on there, too, if anything comes up that you need us to know right away."

Burton laughed. "Not that these NORAID people are going to be giving you a bomb or anything."

"You dropped it in the harbor and ran away?" McGuire said. "You are a girl with real balls, for sure."

"Thanks...I think," Megan responded.

"Okay," Burton said. "You probably need to start work soon. Let's go over to your place and look at those documents of yours. Officially, we have to confirm who you are."

"Okay," Megan agreed. She was glad she had told them the real story and her real name. "But I don't have anything that'll say I was with the IRA."

"We wouldn't expect they would have given you an ID card." Burton shrugged, then thought for a moment. "We're not Customs and Immigration. I'm not sure how they do that, but I guess you'll need something for the asylum part of the deal. We'll have to look into that."

*Right. All ya have to do is call Finian O'Farrell's grandfather somewhere in Armaugh, or Hugh McConnell in his dirty little cellar in Belfast.*

They all walked together to the garage where Megan's apartment was on the second floor, and she got her documents for them.

"Keep the driver's license," McGuire said. He handed it back. We'll just hold on to your passport for a while. Anyone wants to see it, you just call us. We'll take care of whatever it is."

"Okay," Megan said, though the idea of giving up her passport felt uncomfortable to her.

"Now, don't go having any ideas about disappearing on us like you did with the IRA," Burton said.

"I won't," Megan assured them quickly. "You're offering me a way to work legal. Everyone else says I should just marry any old skuzzy guy. I'm definitely going to take your deal."

"Good." Burton smiled.

They extended their hands, and she shook them both.

Then they all walked back to the restaurant, and the agents left in their car.

Erin was there when Megan re-entered the restaurant. She and John came right over to Megan. "What was that all about?" they both demanded.

"Oh, I don't think I can tell you everything about that," she said. "Let me just say they were federal agents, but I'm okay for now. So's the boss, so don't tell her about it. In fact I'm going to be fine, if I do what they say."

"God, what a woman of mystery," John complained.

"She talks to fairies, too," Erin said.

"It's the law; you gotta serve them just as well as normal people these days," John said.

"No, not that kind of fairy." Erin laughed.

"We have magical ones in Ireland," Megan put in. "I'll have t' tell ya all about it some day."

Chapter Twenty-Five

Megan felt a lot more at ease when she walked into Clancy's again. She was a spy all over again, but this was a bar full of pretty much Americans of all kinds of ancestry, no Prods, and certainly no British soldiers. She could hardly believe she might get herself a Green Card for such an easy job.

The bar and the crowd seemed the same as it had before. The donation jars were on the bar and on various tables around the room. The same three singers were just about to start their first set. Megan spotted Sam right away. He smiled at her, and Megan joined him at an empty spot by the bar.

"I came back here," Sam said.

"And I did too." Megan smiled.

"So your friends left you on your own again tonight?"

"They did," Megan lied. "I came for a little taste o' home, don't ya know."

"Can I buy you an Irish beer?" Sam asked.

"Sure," Megan agreed.

Sam waved to the bartender. It was the guy named Patrick, just as before. He came down the bar and took Sam's order for a Guinness for Megan and a refill of the same for him.

"Glad to see ya back," Patrick said to Megan. He said it in a way that made her sense he was really happy that she came.

He moved away to get their drinks, and out of the corner of her eye Megan noticed he went to a phone and made a quick call before filling their glasses at the Guinness tap. *Hmm, I should be friendly to him, and maybe I can meet the singers. They seem to be the most involved with the collections.*

Sam spoke up and distracted her from her thoughts. "Actually I've spent a lot of time down in Texas," he said. "It's a completely different world from Long Island and New York, different as from Ireland to here, I'm sure. They have this stuff down there called Lone Star Beer. I love the stuff, but you can't get it on draft in any Irish bar I've been to."

"Ya don't say." Megan smiled again.

Patrick returned with their drinks.

"I don't see my picture up on the mirror," Megan said to Patrick. She squinted, trying to see all the pictures from where she sat.

"Oh, I haven't got that far with yours." Patrick laughed. He gave a nod and moved away.

"Let's have a reunion toast," Sam said after they had been served. "You give an Irish one, and I'll give an American."

Megan raised her glass. "Up the Republic," she said.

Sam raised his and said, "God bless America."

They each took a sip. Then their attention was attracted by the singer without the top hat who was speaking into his microphone.

"Federal regulations require me to inform any British citizens here tonight that there are life jackets under your seats, and you are all required to wear hard hats."

There was some laughter around the room. The group then launched into a singing of "God Save the Queen." There was more laughter and a few shouts of "Up the Republic" from the crowd. Then for a second verse they sang the American song with the same tune, "My Country, 'Tis of Thee." There was laughter and applause. Someone shouted, "God bless the rising of 1776!"

Megan frowned. "I've never heard those words," she said to Sam.

"It's a song called "America," Sam said. "Every kid learns that in elementary school."

After the song was finished, the singer with the top hat asked, "Does anyone know how t' do CPR on a British soldier?"

Someone shouted back, "No."

"Good!" the singer said, and the group launched into the rousing rebel song about the boys marching at dawn.

Megan and Sam listen to the singing for a while and sipped their beer. Then Patrick suddenly appeared across the bar from her, and Megan felt a presence from behind. She looked around. There were four big men surrounding her and Sam. She spun back around and looked at Patrick.

"This is Megan, here," Patrick said. It was addressed to the men behind her. "Says she's Irish. Says she's from Monheghan."

"So, she does?" one of the men said.

Megan spun around and looked at the one who had spoken. There was no friendliness in his tone. "My name's Tommy, an' these are my friends," he said. The rest of them did not look friendly either.

"Pleased to meet you, I'm sure." Sam smiled. Megan wanted him to stay quiet.

"Pleasure's all ours." Tommy smiled at him. "If ya wouldn't mind, we need t' have a word with Megan, here… Nothin' personal, but it's just between us an' her, ya see." Then he looked back at Megan. "Would ya mind steppin' outside with us for just a minute, dear?"

Megan looked at Sam. "If I'm not back in five minutes, come get me," she said.

"Okay," Sam agreed. His face showed he was not sure of what was going on.

Megan led the way out the door, and she stopped just outside. She turned to face the four men. She didn't want to admit it, but she knew very well who they must be.

Tommy continued to be the spokesman for the group. "So, Megan's your name, but I think you're from Armaugh, not Monheghan."

"What if I am?" Megan demanded, now Americanized enough to be immediately defiant.

"There's a Thomas O'Farrell in Armaugh who wants real bad t' talk to you…"

*Shit. Finian O'Farrell's grandfather, for sure.* It felt like all her insides turned over. She was ready to fight and run. Kick them where it would hurt and run like hell. But she held off, since none of them had yet circled behind her to cut off a possible escape.

"We sent the picture Patrick took of you over there, an' they made a positive identification," Tommy said.

"That bastard…"

"O'Farrell says you left town without completin' a job they gave you…"

"What if I did?" Megan asked. "I'm American now."

The men laughed. One of them said, "An' dearie, so are we."

"Maybe because o' that, we're not gonna do it," Tommy said. "But O'Farrell wants us t' shoot ya in the knees."

Megan's insides felt like they turned over again. "That bastard," she managed to say again.

"Now, we don't know all the details that made 'im want t' order that," Tommy continued. "But we got a job that would be just perfect for you. We told 'im, an' he agreed. If ya do this job for us, he won't want ya shot in the knees."

"What job?" Megan asked.

Tommy glanced around before he spoke again in a much lower tone. "Seems there's a ceremony goin' on at the veteran's cemetery in Calverton, just down the road a piece. Some Yank soldier from World War Two was buried there a few months ago. Seems he saved a couple of British soldiers in the war. They got a unit comin' over here t' lay a wreath or do some shit at 'is grave next Friday. We got a genuine bomb maker from Belfast flyin' in on a tourist visa just in time. Last thing they'd suspect is a pretty young girl like you carryin' a backpack... Gotta show them Brits they're not safe no matter where they are."

Megan was truly speechless.

"That unit was in Belfast not long ago," one of the men added. "Shootin' our people with rubber bullets an' doin' other nasty shit."

"We'll pick ya up here an' drop ya off at the gates of the cemetery," Tommy went on. "You just figure out where they're gonna be, and ya leave the pack on the ground an' get away. All ya have t' do. Then you're home free."

Megan was still speechless. *No preliminaries this time. They just give me a damn bomb.*

"There's an Irish bar near there," Tommy continued. "We can meet there after an' have a pint t' celebrate. Then we'll drive ya back here."

"Yeah, a pint or two." One of the other men laughed.

Megan realized her mouth had dropped open. She shut it and stared back at them for a long moment. *I'll get my damn Green Card. I'm turnin' these bastards in.*

They were interrupted when Sam came out the door. "Hey, you okay?" he asked. "What's going on out here?"

"Oh, these guys just happen to know some of the same people I know back home," Megan said. "They're from Armaugh, just up the road from where I live in Monheghan." The different sides of the border of the two places had no effect on Sam.

Tommy let stand what she had said. He ignored Sam and spoke directly to Megan. "Okay, bright an' early Friday mornin', nine o'clock, right here."

"Okay," Megan agreed. "I'll be here."

"Good." Tommy smiled. He glanced at Sam, then back at Megan. "Why don't we let you an' your friend here get back t' your conversation. We'll have ourselves a pint or two at one o' the tables an' enjoy the music."

"Up the Republic!" one of them put in. And they all laughed.

"Who are those guys?" Sam asked again as he and

Megan walked back into the bar.

"People who know people I know." Megan stuck to her story. "There's some guy's buried down in your veteran's cemetery in Calverton has a connection to Ireland. They thought his family'd like to meet me. It's nothing that would interest you."

"Oh," Sam said, but it was obvious he didn't understand.

"Thanks for comin' out like that to check on me." Megan smiled. Her feelings were sincere.

"I'd do that for any of my friends," Sam said.

"That's good to know," Megan replied. "The next round's on me."

"Sure," Sam agreed.

They returned to their drinks, and they remained silent for a while as the singers continued through their set. Megan looked at her watch. There was still time before Erin would be back to pick her up. She was anxious to call the emergency number on the card the two agents had given her. The singers ended their set, and they did pretty much the same request for funds for the "widows and children" in Northern Ireland as they had the time she was there before. Megan and Sam both passed the hat without adding anything to it again.

During the break, Megan asked, "What's an American war hero funeral like? Do ya know?"

Sam shrugged. "My uncle was a colonel, fought in France or somewhere over there in the Second World War. He had a big military funeral when I was a kid."

"What was it like?" Megan asked.

"Well, they always cover the casket with an American flag. Then they make a big deal of folding it into a triangle, just so." He demonstrated with his hands. "Then they present it to a member of the family. My aunt kept it in the bottom drawer of her dresser till she died. Someone in the family still has it, I'm sure."

"I'm sure they don't have a bagpiper, and a great oration, and hooded men firing rifle salutes into the air," Megan said.

"Sometimes bagpipes." Sam shrugged. He looked at her as if he had no idea of the oration or masked rebels disguising their identities with balaclavas at a funeral. "But I don't think they normally do the rest. Pretty much always a bugler plays 'Taps.' If it's somebody really important, they get 'em there on a horse-drawn gun carriage, and they have a riderless horse following with a pair of boots put in the stirrups backwards."

Megan was then the one who didn't understand. "We all have our different traditions," she said.

"Are you going to a funeral with those guys Friday?"

"Not a funeral," Megan answered. "Some kind of ceremony, though. Our customs are so different sometimes. I was just wondering how it was done over here."

Sam's expression showed that he was not at all interested. "Enough of all this talk about death," he said.

"Right." Megan smiled. "How many of our dead heroes are the rebel songs about?"

"Okay, you got me there." Sam laughed. "But, hey, next week why don't you meet me at some other kind of bar?"

Megan couldn't come up with a quick answer to that.

"You like Mexican food? Ever had a margarita? They have this *Dos Equis* beer from Mexico. It's dark as your Guinness, and, to me, just as damn good."

"But you keep comin' here, an' drinking Guinness?"

"I told you, I love the music." Sam shrugged. "Despite all the dead heroes they sing about an' all… I know, I'm a Texas cowboy at heart, but that south-of-the-border sound just doesn't do a thing for me."

Before she could answer, the singers returned to the stage. Megan slowly sipped her beer through their next set, and she pretended to be as intently listening to the songs of rebel heroes and leaving Ireland as Sam was. Her mind was racing, going over the scene she had just been a part of outside with the strange men. They remained at a table not far away, drinking several rounds of the good dark beer.

Just as it was about time for Erin to be coming by, Sam excused himself and headed for the men's room. Megan took the opportunity to quickly slip away. The four men remained at their table and did not immediately follow her out the door. But she saw the one who called himself Tommy come out the door as Erin drove her away.

\*\*\*\*

"How'd it go?" Erin asked when they were on the road, as she had the time before.

"I truly don't know," Megan answered simply.

"Any good marriage prospects talk to you? That's something you can talk about, can't you? Or do you need to go running and talk to those fairies of yours again before you give me an answer?"

"Ah, yes, my fairies." Megan smiled. "Sure an'

they an' I have a lot t' talk about right now."

"I was a fairy once, in a school play."

"All in good time. I promise I will tell you quite a story, maybe after this coming Friday."

Erin gave her a look that said she absolutely didn't understand what was going on.

"I promise," Megan repeated. "Like you Americans say, cross my heart and hope to die."

"I'm gonna hold you to that," Erin said.

They drove on in silence for a while. When they reached the main road on the way to where Megan lived, she noticed Erin was looking in her mirror much more than usual.

"I think there's a car following us," Erin suddenly said.

Megan looked around, suddenly alert. "It's those bastards from the bar," she announced. "These four guys were hittin' on me, an I gave 'em what for. They must want to know where I live."

"Bastards," Erin agreed. "That's happened to me before, too."

The car suddenly started going faster, and a determined expression crossed Erin's face as she concentrated entirely on the road. Megan kept watching the headlights behind them.

"Don't worry," Erin said. "I know all the back roads around here. We all used to make out in the orchards an' drink an' shit, when we were in high school. I'll get rid of 'em, don't worry."

Megan felt confident they would.

The sporty Camaro suddenly slowed just enough to make a sharp right without turning over, and then gained speed on a pot-holed back road. The car behind them missed the turn, but the two women knew it would turn around and come down the road. On their left were the rows of evenly spaced trees of an orchard. Erin suddenly turned left and went along a short distance on a dirt road among the trees. Then she shut off her lights and killed the engine.

They both looked out the back window and watched and waited as a car passed on the pot-holed road behind them. Erin started up and hurried off along the dirt road. Megan felt anxious, with the car's lights still off, but there was a good three-quarter moon high in the summer sky. That and her familiarity with the road was enough for Erin to get them to another pot-holed back road, where she turned left again and put on her lights. Then they were quickly back on the main road headed home.

Megan kept watch, and she didn't see headlights behind them. Erin came up on a slow-going pickup truck overloaded with old furniture. Megan felt as if her heart leaped into her mouth as Erin passed the truck. Then Erin slowed enough to just stay in front of the truck. "There." She smiled. "We'll easily see anyone who tries to get in between. But I'll bet those stupid bastards are still pokin' around in the old orchard, lookin' for us there."

"Thanks," Megan said.

"No problem." Erin smiled again. "Like I told you, we don't take shit like that any more."

"Yes," Megan agreed. "Thanks again."

Chapter Twenty-Six

Burton and McGuire responded right away to the conversation Megan had with the agent who answered the emergency number. As she arrived at the restaurant the next morning, they pulled in the driveway.

"We had no idea you'd come up with a report like that," Burton said as they hustled up to where she had stopped just short of the door.

"Good job, my God," McGuire said.

"Okay, come in," Megan said. "There are no customers here yet. We can have coffee and sit far away from anyone who might hear."

"Too much coffee is never enough," McGuire agreed.

Megan led them in. John was already behind the bar as usual. She took them to a table all the way across the room, by a big picture window. High beach grass, a strip of sand, and the deep blue Peconic Bay were the view on a bright sunny day.

Megan went back to the coffee station between the end of the bar and the door to the kitchen.

The door to the kitchen opened a crack, but no one came out. "Who men?" the Spanish-speaking prep chef asked from the kitchen side.

John heard him. "*Federales,*" he answered in a loud whisper.

"They're not here for you," Megan started to

answer, but the door swung quickly shut on her.

John laughed. "Looks like you're doing prep again today," he said. "That boy's running and probably already past the dumpster out back by now."

"That's not funny," Megan complained. Then she hurried away with the coffees for herself and the two agents.

"This is a fascinating turn of events," Burton said after Megan had served the coffees and sat down with them. "We were worried about the financing of bombs over in Northern Ireland. We weren't thinking about them doing anything like that here."

Megan gave them a quick rundown of all that had happened, just as she had with the agent on the phone the night before. She had called the twenty-four-hour number as soon as she got home.

"Now they got themselves a sudden opportunity," McGuire spoke up. "We were in early, and we did some checking on the information you gave our night agent last night. The British owe a lot to this guy of ours who recently died and was buried in the Calverton Cemetery. He threw a grenade and shot some Germans who would have otherwise surprised and wiped out a group of this British unit in the push across France to liberate Paris." McGuire paused and produced a notebook from his pocket. He flipped a few pages and continued. "So there's a company from this same unit, today's soldiers who are in it, of course, coming over here to train in Texas in some NATO joint training. They're going to stop here and be in a ceremony to honor this guy, lay a wreath on his grave, film it for the folks back home..." McGuire squinted at his notes. "This sergeant from our side was a Bradley Smith."

"At least it's not an Irish-sounding name." Burton laughed.

"That's America for you," McGuire said to Megan. "People of all ancestries in our army here." He looked back at his notes. "Anyway, this British unit that's coming is from the Queen's Own Sixty-First Highlanders, and…"

"What!" Megan exclaimed.

"The army press guy told me it's the Queen's Own Sixty-First Highlanders," McGuire said again. "You've heard of them?"

At first Megan couldn't find her voice. Then she said, all in a rush, "They were the ones that hung out in the pub in Belfast where I was supposed to leave the bomb."

"Oh, my God!" Burton exclaimed. "Maybe these guys who approached you are more sophisticated than we think."

"You think they actually connected that?" McGuire asked him. "A troop of British soldiers is a great target, no matter what unit they're from."

"True," Burton said. "But it's like instead of shooting her in the knees for tossing their bomb in the harbor, they send her back to blow up the same unit she may have saved in Ireland."

Megan let that sink in. *Is Andrew going to be with them?* The question filled her mind.

"This turn of events is actually really good for you," Burton said. "We won't have to verify your story about why you had to leave Ireland for the asylum thing. If we catch these guys and connect them to the IRA, it'll be obvious that you can't go back safely to Ireland."

"Oh, good." Megan realized what he was saying. "Yes, that's really good."

"Right," McGuire said. "I mean, this bomb thing is a complete surprise. But someone we catch here may well lead us to the trail of money funding the IRA from here or from Ireland. We're still after that, even though you're not someone we'd send into that bar again, after this. The money came from somewhere for the bomb materials, for the bomb maker's plane ticket over here… Stuff like that. You never know where it may lead."

"But we want to catch them after they've given you the bomb," Burton continued. "And after they've driven you to the cemetery. Then it's no question what they're up to. No question that it's international terror aimed at one of the usual targets of the IRA. The bad guys' lawyers won't be able to question a thing."

Megan was listening, but a part of her mind was still stuck on the fact that the British soldiers were going to be from the Queen's Own Sixty-First Highlanders, just like in the Belfast pub.

"They said they'd pick you up Friday at nine in the morning at Clancy's," McGuire said. "So we've come up with a plan. One of our agents will pick you up here and drop you off at Clancy's…"

"Female agent," Burton put in. "She'll have an older car, look like some friend dropping you off, in case they're already there."

"Don't worry, you'll be followed the whole way," McGuire continued. "When they drop you off at the cemetery, you get out and walk away with the bomb. Then we move in on them. Soon as you see us surround their car, you gently put the bomb down. And you run away from it like hell."

"Okay," Megan agreed. "I'm a runner. That part'll be no trouble to me."

"So you think you can do it?" Burton asked.

"I carried a bomb all the way through Belfast from this old lady's house to the harbor," Megan said. "I can take a chance this one won't go off on me either."

"Great," Burton said. "You stay well away while the bomb squad comes and takes care of whatever they give you. We'll catch up to you after we get everything secure."

"Okay." Megan nodded.

"Good," McGuire also said. "Call us if anything comes up before Friday that you think we should know."

"Sure, I will," Megan agreed again.

"Good." Burton stood up. "We'll be off, then. Thanks for the coffee. We've got a lot of things to put in place."

McGuire stood also. He put his notebook away, and the agents went quickly away.

Megan took the empty cups and headed to the kitchen door. Erin and John were waiting for her at the end of the bar.

"I've gotta ask the boss for the day off Friday," Megan said. "I've got a job to do to help these guys out and keep my freedom in the meantime."

"Now, that sounds interesting," Erin said. "Boss is in her office. She said to tell you there's green beans and salads need prepping. That Mexican prep chef seems to be gone."

Megan rolled her eyes. "Guess there'd be no deal for him. I suppose nobody's collecting for widows and children in that Mexican restaurant down the road."

"Can't you tell us what the hell is going on now?" Erin demanded. "Or do you have to talk to those fairies of yours some more?"

"No." Megan shook her head. "I've got to get busy on the prep. No time to talk to any fairies now." She turned away and went on into the kitchen.

"Has she gone balmy on us?" John asked.

"Balmy?"

"Yeah, crazy," he explained. "I think that's how the British say it."

"She's Irish, not British," Erin corrected. "I don't think they're all that much the same."

"*Loco* then." John laughed. "*La senorita es muy loco,* or, as we Americans say, crazier 'n a shit house rat."

"Yes, a little bit crazy," Erin agreed. "Crazy, for sure."

## Chapter Twenty-Seven

The woman who picked up Megan on Friday morning introduced herself simply as Agent Dempsey. She was just a bit older than Megan, and dressed the same, casually, like any of the summer people that were all about. She was obviously ready to fit in with any crowd they might encounter during the day. Megan wondered if she was carrying a gun.

Dempsey was right on time. She was all business, and Megan sensed a tenseness, like this was a big operation for all of the agents as well as for her. Megan said a quick prayer to her fairies as they drove quickly toward Riverhead and Clancy's bar.

Dempsey suddenly spoke up. "We've got a lot of agents assigned to this today," she said. "We might be stopping an international incident, after all."

Megan's feelings about the tenseness were confirmed.

"We even have a bomb squad waiting at the nearest fire station," Dempsey continued. "The cemetery's been swept, and it's been under surveillance all night. We think we're ready for anything they might throw at us today."

"Wow," Megan said. "America always continues to impress me."

"Don't worry," Dempsey assured her. "Soon as I drop you, we'll have you in our sight all the way."

"Good," Megan agreed. *A lot different here than the way I was dropped with a bomb in Belfast.* But the assurance that a number of the agents would be watching out for her didn't make Megan feel any more at ease.

Tommy and the same three men were waiting in front of Clancy's when Megan arrived. They were gathered around a big Ford sedan, the sole car in the parking lot at that hour of the day. They all wore sunglasses and were dressed in summer clothes just as if they had been on Long Island all the time. Dempsey stopped in front of where they stood. Megan got out and started toward the men. She paused a moment and turned to wave a thanks to Dempsey as if she were a friend who had given her a ride. The agent was already moving away.

"Top o' the mornin' to ya," Tommy said with a wide grin. "'Tis a pleasure t' see ya again, I'm sure." The other men were smiling and nodding as well.

"Yes, a pleasure," Megan agreed, but she did not smile. She wondered if any of them would bring up the fact that Erin lost them on the way home from the bar.

"Come, then," Tommy said. "We want t' be there in plenty of time." His mind was obviously focused on the task at hand.

One of the men opened the back door of the car for her. He gestured for her to get in, with a nod of his head. Megan complied. She realized there was a backpack on the floor as she slid across the seat to the center. It looked pretty much like the ones she had carried in Ireland. This one was a pretty shade of muted red.

"Be careful of that pack," the man who had held

the door said as he climbed in behind her.

"Right," Megan replied.

One of the other men got in the rear seat from the other side. They sandwiched her and the bomb between them. *No escape now.* She stifled a sudden feeling of panic. *Maybe it's not a bomb in there. Maybe they're going to take me into the woods and shoot me, instead.*

Tommy got in the front and drove.

They pulled out of the lot and headed away. Megan looked around as they passed a couple of nondescript but occupied parked cars. The occupants seemed to ignore them passing, but Megan was sure at least one of them was there for her. It made her feel a little better. She looked in the mirror over the dash. It was turned so she could really see only Tommy as he drove. She knew very well that she couldn't look around to see what cars were behind them. They drove along in silence for a while.

Tommy spoke up. "Ready today for this?" he asked.

"Yes," Megan answered. "I'm ready."

The man on her left reached over and pointed to a stray strap that was sticking out of the pack. "You pull this, love, when you've set it down," he said. He did not try to fake a pull to demonstrate. "Then ya got ten minutes to just kind o' wander away."

"Right," Megan said. She was struck by the similarity to the workings of the bomb she had been given in Belfast. She had never thought that standardization was any part of the IRA.

"Try t' get as close to the soldiers as ya can," the man on her right said. "The more we get, the better."

"Still, don't do anything t' make yourself

noticeable, of course," the man on her left said.

"Right," Megan agreed again. "How far do I need t' be away?"

"Far as ya can," the man on the right said. "Ten minutes should be more than enough t' give ya plenty o' distance an' time."

"Okay, good," Megan said, though she definitely had a different plan.

"Hang around after it's done," Tommy said from the front seat. "We'll come find ya in the crowd."

"Okay," Megan agreed again. She was wondering if any of them were going to bring up the bomb in Belfast and give her a warning that she had better go through with it this time.

Tommy took the conversation a completely different way. "That guy you were with in the bar the other night, he your boyfriend?"

"Sort of," Megan answered.

"Ah, so 'sort of' kind o' means half way," Tommy said. "That would mean you're halfway unattached, as well."

"It doesn't mean that," Megan objected.

"Pretty girl like you," Tommy said. "That's a damn shame, if ya be askin' me…"

"Aren't we almost there?" Megan asked, impatient.

"Yeah, I think it's right down the road here," Tommy said. "I suppose you've got a lot on your mind right now besides attachments." He gave a disappointed sigh.

Megan said a quick prayer to her fairies. She was ready to plant a bomb, if it would get her out of the car and away from these men. Then she saw a directional sign for Calverton Cemetery. "There's a sign," she said, and she pointed to it.

"So it is." Tommy nodded. He followed the direction indicated by the sign. "Let's all say a quick prayer t' the great Saint Patrick for the success o' your mission."

"Yes," Megan agreed, even though her fairies had answered the prayer she had prayed.

"Good Saint Patrick, please help her on her sacred mission this day," Tommy prayed.

The man on Megan's right added, "And may all of Ireland be free."

Then they all said, "Amen."

Megan remained silent. *Are these guys for real?*

The car passed through the cemetery gate and swung around a car full of men sitting just inside.

*Bet they're part of the crew that's here for me.* Again she felt better. *Thank you, fairies, Saint Patrick, or whoever...*

Tommy pulled over on the grass on the side of the drive. Rows of grave markers stretched across green grass all around. Tommy indicated a group of spectators and two groups of uniformed soldiers a distance away. "There they are." He gestured with his head.

The crowd was obviously made up mostly of veterans and their families. Some of them had uniforms of the American veteran organizations. The US Army group included a band. They were decked out in their dark blue dress uniforms. The British had the traditional bright red coats and black bearskin headgear. They were wearing the same colors as they had when they were adversaries in colonial times. Megan thought it quite impressive.

The man to her right got out of the back seat and held the door for her. Megan lifted the backpack by its handle from the car floor. "Wish me Godspeed," she said, now totally into her role. She slid across the seat and got out. She stepped away so the man could get back into the rear seat. As she did, Megan saw, out of the corner of her eye, a car coming quickly toward them. She looked around and saw another car coming from the opposite direction. Megan walked a few feet, still holding the backpack by the canvas handle on top. She heard Tommy pull away behind her. Then there was more than one squeal of brakes, with slamming of car doors. She kept walking and did not look around.

"FBI! Get out of that car and keep your hands up!" she heard an authoritative voice order.

Megan set the backpack gently down on the grass in the aisle between the grave markers. Then she ran.

She ran toward the soldiers in the red coats. Reaching them was all she now wanted to do. Suddenly, uniformed local police appeared, running toward the spectators and soldiers too.

"Move back, everyone!" the police were shouting. "We may have a bomb."

Megan was close enough to the British soldiers to hear an officer shout, "Break ranks, move back!" to the men. The American soldiers did the same. All was chaos for a few moments as everyone moved back as the police were ordering.

Megan mixed into the confusion and got among the soldiers, but it was hard to distinguish one from another with them all in the same uniform and headgear.

"Andrew!" she called.

One of the soldiers looked around. It was him.

Megan smiled.

Andrew stared at her for a moment. Then he recognized her. "Sarah?" he said. "What are you doing here?"

They stood facing each other, both too shocked to even embrace.

"The reason I didn't come back to the pub and the reason I'm here today are the same," Megan said. "I've got a bit of a story t' tell ya, if you're willin' t' listen?"

A policeman ordered everyone farther back, and Megan and Andrew walked together in the crowd.

"This way, lads," a sergeant shouted to his men.

"I got your letter," Andrew said as they both moved along. They ignored all the questions and talk about a bomb and the confusion going on around them.

"You got me flowers," Megan said. "I still owe you a night o' dancin'."

"Yes, you do," he agreed. "Yes, you do."

"Unless you'd rather shoot me with that gun you're carryin'."

He laughed. "They're not loaded for this kind of thing. Even the lads who fire the salute have blanks."

"I like that." She smiled.

"They're giving us two days off to see New York," he said. "I'm sure there's a place to go dancin' there."

"Yes, there're many."

The crowd had stopped moving. Megan and Andrew stopped, too. The police had somehow determined everyone was a safe enough distance away. "We got a bomb squad checkin' it out, folks," one of the policemen yelled. "There will be just a short delay."

"Detail form up!" the British sergeant ordered.

"I gotta go," Andrew said. "The lads are talkin'

about goin' to this place calls itself a British pub just down the road tonight. It's called the Keg of Ale."

"I'll find it," Megan promised. "And this time I'll show."

"Around nine," he added. "I want to hear your story why…" The sergeant began barking orders, and Andrew moved quickly away.

The British soldiers marched over to join the blue-coated American troops. Then they all stood at ease in facing formations as their officers discussed what next to do.

Megan was startled back to reality when Agent Dempsey appeared in front of her. "Great job!" Dempsey said. For the first time that day she had a smile.

Megan still felt kind of numb.

"You've got to come to the office now," Dempsey continued. "We need you to tell your story so we can write up an affidavit for you to sign."

"Okay," Megan agreed. "Just so it doesn't take longer than nine tonight."

Dempsey laughed. "By then, I'll probably have gone to bed. You know how early they had me up this morning?" She didn't answer that question but added, "Don't worry, we're not going to say anything more to the papers and TV than that you're an 'unnamed informant.' We are definitely not going to advertise what you did today to the world and the IRA."

"Thanks," Megan said. She hadn't even thought of that.

"You may have saved a lot of lives," Dempsey said as if it were simply a fact.

Megan hadn't actually thought of that, either. *And*

*Andrew has no idea about that yet. No more secrets. I'm gonna start by telling him my real name.*

"I've got a favor to ask," she said. "There's a pub down the road from here called the Keg of Ale. When we're finished, can you drop me off there?"

"Sure," Dempsey agreed. "You earned yourself a lot more than a ride to a pub."

They started walking away from all the commotion and toward where Dempsey had parked her car. Megan looked around. It was a bright sunny day. The green grass and grave markers stretched in all directions. There were a few scattered trees. Megan didn't know exactly what she was feeling. It wasn't the Irish countryside, but maybe she was finally feeling the presence of her fairies after all.

Chapter Twenty-Eight

Erin came by early in her car for the ride she had agreed to give Megan to Kennedy Airport. Two months had passed since Megan had disrupted the IRA bombing attempt in Calverton. She now had her Green Card, and Andrew had two weeks' leave from his unit. Megan had a round-trip plane ticket to Scotland. She was going to meet him and see his hometown.

"I still can't believe all the stuff you told me," Erin said as she drove along. The American music Megan was now so used to was playing on the car radio.

"All true," Megan said. "I promised myself—now I'm legal, I won't lie any more. Not ever."

"All that stuff on TV about the bomb, and you're still an 'unnamed informant.' " You probably saved a lot of people."

"Believe me, I want it to be that way. I never wanted to be a hero. I just want to be a girl who likes to run across the countryside and have a nice man and home to run back to."

"God, don't we all." Erin smiled. "The man and the home, I mean. I don't run… You really think you got the man part of it, huh?"

"When we went dancin' in New York City and spent the night together in a hotel, I told him everything. He says he doesn't care I was with the IRA, since I changed my ways and messed up their bomb plans. Now we're gonna spend two weeks together in his hometown. We are gonna see how it works, for sure… I mean, he's a British soldier, and I'm an Irish Catholic. We agreed t' take it slow, and see."

"Are you sure you're going to be safe from those people who gave you the bomb?"

"I'm probably safer in a small town in Scotland where everybody knows each other than here with all the summer people and Irish bars."

"Clancy's has been closed since those guys talked, and they arrested the bartender, too."

"He was such an asshole." Megan dismissed him with a wave of her hand. "Took my picture without askin', then sent it to Ireland to see if they knew who I was."

"Takes all kinds." Erin shrugged. "Just like the customers we serve. We sure get all kinds… You gonna try to get a job as a teacher when you come back?"

"You think the boss'll be upset with that?"

"Yep, you're such a nice person, for bein' so smart, an' all."

"Thanks, I think."

"It's just that you've been to college an' all. You shouldn't be preppin' salads an' waitin' tables all your life," Erin said. "Of course, you do tell us you talk to fairies none of us have ever seen."

"That night I spent with Andrew in New York City was magical. I'm not sure about Scotland. I'm gonna find out. But I'm from Ireland, and Ireland is a magical place." Megan smiled. "And I talk to my fairies. Yes, I do."

## A word about the author…

Bill Lockwood was a social worker by day for the states of Maryland and Vermont until he retired in June of 2015. By night he was an avid amateur theater participant and writer.

He wrote reviews and feature articles in a Baltimore theater newsletter, had four short stories published in obscure literary magazines in the early 1990s, wrote articles on the arts, personalities, and rural downtown development in the "Bellows Falls Town Crier" in Vermont from the late 1990s through 2006.

He also wrote articles in Vermont tourist publications and other small papers. In 2006 he was Greater Falls Regional Chamber of Commerce Person of the Year in recognition of his work as Chairman of the Bellows Falls Opera House Restoration Committee.

In the mid 1980s, he was a frequent visitor to Long Island, where his wife's family had a home and where this story is partly set. His own family has Irish heritage.

His first novel, *Buried Gold*, was published by The Wild Rose Press in August 2016. This is his second novel.

Thank you for purchasing
this publication of The Wild Rose Press, Inc.

If you enjoyed the story, we would appreciate your
letting others know by leaving a review.

For other wonderful stories,
please visit our on-line bookstore at
www.thewildrosepress.com.

For questions or more information
contact us at
info@thewildrosepress.com.

The Wild Rose Press, Inc.
www.thewildrosepress.com

Stay current with The Wild Rose Press, Inc.

Like us on Facebook

https://www.facebook.com/TheWildRosePress

And Follow us on Twitter
https://twitter.com/WildRosePress